Stitches

Glen Huser

A GROUNDWOOD BOOK
DOUGLAS & McINTYRE
TORONTO VANCOUVER BERKELEY

Copyright © 2003 by Glen Huser
Third printing 2004

No part of this publication may be reproduced, stored in a retrieval system
or transmitted, in any form or by any means, without the prior written
consent of the publisher or a licence from The Canadian Copyright
Licensing Agency (Access Copyright). For an Access Copyright licence,
visit www.accesscopyright.ca or call toll free to
1-800-893-5777.

Groundwood Books / Douglas & McIntyre
720 Bathurst Street, Suite 500, Toronto, Ontario M5S 2R4

Distributed in the USA by Publishers Group West
1700 Fourth Street, Berkeley, CA 94710

We acknowledge for their financial support of our publishing program the
Canada Council for the Arts, the Government of Canada through the
Book Publishing Industry Development Program (BPIDP), the Ontario
Arts Council and the Government of Ontario through the Ontario Media
Development Corporation's Ontario Book Initiative.

ONTARIO ARTS COUNCIL
CONSEIL DES ARTS DE L'ONTARIO

The Alberta
Foundation
for the Arts

Alberta
COMMUNITY DEVELOPMENT

COMMITTED TO THE DEVELOPMENT OF CULTURE AND THE ARTS

National Library of Canada Cataloging in Publication
Huser, Glen
Stitches / by Glen Huser.
ISBN 0-88899-553-9 (bound).–ISBN 0-88899-578-4 (pbk.)
I. Title.
PS8565.U823S73 2003   jC813'.54   C2003-902083-5
PZ7

Cover illustration by Betsy Everitt
Design by Michael Solomon

Printed and bound in Canada

Stitches

This book is dedicated, with love,
to the Daily sisters:
Beatrice Huser and Orene Miller

One

Midsummer.

Those hot nights at the tail end of July, thunderstorms rolled across Acton. I'd crawl out of bed and look out over the roofs of the trailer court, shiny from rain. Sheet lightning would flash, silhouetting the buildings of the town stretched along the horizon – a couple of church spires, three grain elevators, the TV booster aerial with its tiny red lights strung on metal crosshatching.

Mavis Buttley Junior High wasn't something you'd pick out along the skyline, but it was what was on my mind that summer between grades six and seven. Sometimes, at two o'clock in the morning, with thunder grumbling in the distance, I'd try to imagine what my life would be like six weeks in the future, or six months down the road.

I already knew junior high was a whole different world from Acton Elementary, the only school I'd gone to so far. On orientation day in June we'd seen some of it: the long hallways lined with lockers, kids spilling out of classrooms as buzzers sounded, surging off in different directions – to the computer lab, the shop, the home ec room, the library. Chantelle had grabbed hold of my arm and said, "A person could get trampled in this stampede."

There were no recess breaks. That's a good thing if you've been the victim of schoolyard bullies most of your life. The less free time for Shon Docker and his gang to pick on you, the better.

The thought of going into grade seven was scary in lots of ways, but going nowhere was worse. I wanted to be there in the middle of it all. I could feel the tug of my life ahead of me, the pull of places to go, things to do.

As if it would make the summer go faster, I made the trip into town at least once a day to meet Chantelle. My feet knew every rut in the gravel road that cut from the trailer court through a stretch of trees and along a farmer's field before connecting up to the main highway. In midsummer, insects moved lazily over the dusty weeds and wildflowers. Sometimes a mouse or a gopher scurried through the ditch grass.

Once I got to Acton, my running shoes always seemed to find their way to the avenue where Mavis Buttley stretched over most of a block. The school looked like a giant shoebox that had been covered with old porridge. Paint around the windows, a brownish-red that made me think of dried blood, was beginning to flake, showing bits of green. Pine green had been the color of the trim when Gentry, my mom, and Kitaleen, my aunt, had gone there twenty years ago.

"Maybe we could run away," Chantelle suggested when she met me there in front of the building.

She was kidding, of course. Chantelle couldn't run anywhere.

"Sounds like a good idea," I said. "Do you think there's a place where there are no Shon Dockers?"

That would be heaven. A place where you could do what you wanted and no one would make fun of you. Where your best friend could be a girl. Where people wouldn't look away when they saw someone like Chantelle.

No one could say life had been easy for Chantelle. She had scars. The one cutting diagonally across her upper lip was the most noticeable, of course. "A hare lip," Kitaleen called it. "That poor girl. She didn't need a hare lip on top of everything else."

People could hardly ever talk about Chantelle without slipping in something about "that poor girl."

"They say her mama never wanted her to be born," Kitaleen told me. "They say Eva Boscombe tried to, you know, get rid of her but she was too far along. And when she was born – oh, my..." Kitaleen's hand fluttered along her chest. "Well, everyone could see she was too tiny and all scrunched out of shape. Dora Jenkins was on the night shift over at the hospital and she said she'd never seen such an ugly baby."

I knew Chantelle had heard all these stories.

"People think because I'm small, I can't understand what they're saying," she once told me. "That if they whisper, the sound won't reach my ears." She looked up at me and laughed – that laugh as thin and wispy as dandelion seeds on the wind.

There were many stories about Chantelle. One was that Eva Boscombe, after bringing an even half dozen children into the world (no one ever said she raised them – the Boscombe boys more or less raised themselves), was sure she'd reached the point where she was past having babies. Chantelle proved she was wrong about that.

And then there was the story that Ed Boscombe wasn't really Chantelle's father.

"If you ask me," Gentry liked to say, "more than half the section crew, that vacuum-cleaner salesman who drove the sea-blue sedan and Doug Penfield down at the Esso station were all looking a little pale round the gills when word got out that Eva was in the family way." Then Gentry would whoop her laugh – that laugh people liked to hear when she was running a bit of patter between her songs. "Guess you might say Eva was more in the community way."

Kitaleen would cluck her tongue and try to hush my mom. "You shouldn't spread those stories. In the end they could hurt that child and she looks like she's been hurt enough already." Kitaleen could chew on a good bit of gossip herself, but she'd get mad at the way Gentry liked to tell the whole world about everything without ever thinking how it might affect people.

"Maybe the Boscombe boys grew up like weeds," Kitaleen decided, "but Eva does lavish attention on Chantelle."

"The way you do with a dog or cat," Gentry added.

It was true. It was an odd kind of care, almost as if Chantelle were a special pet. And it wasn't just Eva. Most grownups treated her that way. It seemed to me that they were surprised when Chantelle actually spoke.

But then Chantelle always chose carefully the people she would talk to.

I was one of the chosen.

Chantelle and I started school together in grade one. I don't remember her talking at all back then. It wasn't that she couldn't speak. She simply chose not to.

A lot of the time her desk would be empty. She was

often away sick or off in the city for corrective surgery. When she did come to school, kids stared at her face, and some of them giggled over the funny way she walked. Once, when Chantelle was away in grade two, our teacher, Miss Thwarpe, talked to us about teasing someone less fortunate than ourselves.

"Chantelle is not a dummy and you must never call her that," she said, looking directly at Todd Wingate and Cameron Coaldale.

The two squirmed and glanced sideways at each other before looking down at the floor. But some of it must have sunk in, because even after Chantelle came back with her legs in braces, they left her alone and came after me instead. They had a special name for me, too. It was girlie.

When I came home in tears, Kitaleen would chant softly, "Sticks and stones may break my bones but names will never hurt me."

Neither of us said anything to Gentry. We knew that Gentry would fly down to the school, scream, holler and threaten, and then disappear like a spent tornado, leaving others to deal with the wreckage.

Kitaleen would cuddle me to her and stroke my hair along my forehead. "Consider the source," she'd say as a backup to her sticks-and-stones chant. No matter how pregnant she was (and it seemed that my aunt was always expecting one baby or another), she was always able to fit me in for a hug.

Then she'd find something for us to snack on. "Oh, my," she'd giggle. "There's not much that melted marshmallows won't cure."

It wasn't until we were in grade five that Chantelle finally talked at school, and the first person she spoke to was me.

The team of Todd Wingate and Cameron Coaldale had grown to include Shon Docker. Shon was older than us – he must have repeated a grade at some point – and he liked to do more than just call people names. Chantelle was watching the day Todd and Cameron held my arms while Shon pulled off my pants at recess, shrieking at the sight of my pink jockey shorts.

The shorts, of course, hadn't been pink when we bought them, just your basic Stanfield white. But laundry was not one of Kitaleen's strengths, and a red sweater had colored an entire load of whites so that everything came out pink. Shon discovered my secret as we changed for gym one day, and it was his torture of choice to trap me in the schoolyard once the teacher on supervision was around the corner and expose me to as much of the school population as possible.

"Pink panties," Todd would holler, almost choking on his laughter. "Girlie's wearing pink panties!"

I ended up crying every time. I wished I could have been tough, at least tough enough not to cry, but I wasn't.

After one of these attacks, Chantelle trekked across the tarmac to where I was hurrying back into my pants. I could see her coming. She had a walk like no one else, a kind of glide interrupted with lurches, as she struggled to get her balance every few steps. She glided, dipped and dived her way over to me.

"You make it too easy," she said.

I was so startled to hear her talk that I made some half-human noise like "Wha...?"

"You need to wear things that aren't so easy to pull off," she whispered. "And you need some white underwear."

For some reason I began crying harder than ever, tears streaming along my cheeks and trickling saltily into my mouth.

And then Chantelle reached down, her small hand clutching my shoulder. "Hush," she said. Such an odd word for another kid to say. "Don't cry," she added. "I'll help you." In that slightly crooked face with its scarred lip and too-wide mouth, it was her eyes you noticed when she got close. They were beautiful. Violet colored, fringed with heavy dark lashes.

"How come..." I sputtered.

She put a finger to her mouth, motioning me to be

silent. Miss Thwarpe, the teacher on supervision, rounded the corner of the building.

"Travis. Chantelle. Come along, you two," she called. "The bell's gone."

Later, Chantelle dropped a folded piece of paper onto my notebook as she lurched across the library.

Meet me at the Goodwill at 4:30, the note said.

Two years earlier a Goodwill store had been set up in what had been a restaurant on Acton's Main Street. No one had bothered to take the lunch counter out, and its pink mother-of-pearl counter was now dotted with discarded knickknacks.

When I got to the store, Chantelle was perched on top of a lunch-counter stool like some strange little bird.

She smiled and waved me over.

"They got jumpsuits," she said. "Nobody wears jumpsuits but they might be the best thing for you. For a while."

"Jumpsuits?"

"All in one piece. And the good thing is they're just a dollar-fifty each."

"I only got eighty cents," I said.

"A birthday present," she smiled. "We'll get two so you can change. And here's the rest of your present." She handed me the bag she'd been cradling in her lap. It contained a three-pack of boys' briefs. White. She must have stopped at Toggle's on her way to the Goodwill.

"It's not my birthday," I said lamely.

"That's okay. I've missed all of yours so far."

Two

- - - - - - - - - - - - - -

Chantelle was right. It was almost impossible for Shon, even with two helpers, to get me out of a jumpsuit in less than ten minutes. Once they did get it unzipped enough to find out I was wearing white shorts, they lost interest.

There were always other kids to bully. If they felt like it, they'd even pick on kids half their size. On Halloween Chantelle and I saw just how low they'd stoop.

Across from Buttley Park we noticed a couple of little boys sitting at the edge of the road. One, a mummy that had come unraveled, was crying. It looked like he was sitting in a nest of white rags.

I recognized the other boy – Darin Rogers, a kid who lived two trailers over in the trailer park. His plastic Batman costume had been ripped apart.

"What happened?"

"We were robbed." Darin's voice quavered. "Jimmy wouldn't give them his bag and they beated him. They had Scream masks."

"One of them was called Shon," Jimmy said, his voice coming out in fits and starts.

Chantelle shook her head and sighed. We had a pretty small haul of treats ourselves, but we gave them what we had except for two O Henry bars that we ate as the four of us straggled down the street.

I walked the boys back to Darin's trailer and made sure they were inside before going home myself. Kitaleen was alone in the kitchen and I could see she'd been crying, too. There was a small mountain of toffee wrappers scattered on the table in front of her. When she and Miserable Mike fought, it generally ended with my uncle storming out of the house and Kitaleen consoling herself with a good cry and a good-sized snack.

"I swear that man can pick a fight out of thin air." She popped another toffee into her mouth. "Got his tail in a tizzy because we used some of the matches from his old match collection. Just a couple to light the jack-o'-lantern and get a bit of charcoal to go round Ashley's ghost eyes. Lord, I don't think he's looked at those matches in fifteen years. Been sitting in that ugly beer stein collecting dust for as long as I can remember."

Kitaleen unwrapped another toffee.

"He said didn't I have nothing better to do than be playing with matches and goofing around when there was dishes to do and lunches to make. And didn't I know those were his best matches from Chez Pierre? Blah-blah-blah. Wouldn't have been no use telling him I'd been helping the kids carve jack-o'-lanterns and putting the finishing touches on that little princess costume Jasmine had her heart set on. Of course Mike wouldn't take two minutes to help with Halloween himself. Holman wanted to be Harry Potter and we had to go hunting for a broomstick to fix up. That took some time. You know Mike. If he wants to scrap, I can't say nothing."

One time I asked Kitaleen why she'd married Mike. This was after they'd ended an argument by throwing pots and pans at one another. Mike had a better aim than Kitaleen, and he'd raised a good-sized bruise on her left arm, while all she'd managed to do was send a trail of tomato sauce along the tiles above the kitchen sink.

"Lord knows," she sighed. "I guess I wanted babies and he was the only man who came courting. I didn't have looks, you see, like your mom."

I tried to think back to Mike being Kitaleen's boyfriend, but I couldn't remember. I was only four when they got married. There was Kitaleen's wedding and Grandma's funeral in the same year. It was hard to imagine Mike being anyone's boyfriend.

"He used to laugh more," Kitaleen said, as if she'd

read my mind. "And I did have pretty hair." She tossed her head slightly so that her blonde curls rearranged themselves along her shoulders. "Mike wasn't exactly Tom Cruise himself."

Gentry told me her version of it all.

"Talk about a guy sizing things up wrong," she laughed. "Mike thought he was marrying Miss Homemaker of the Year. Of course that was while your grandma was still alive, and Mom did keep things wonderful-like. Not that we ever had two nickels to rub together, but your grandma had a way of filling a house with good cooking smells, and house plants bursting with flowers, and fresh wallpaper." Gentry stopped for a few seconds and I was wishing I could see Grandma's house in my mind. Sometimes I thought I could remember the good cooking smells. Ginger cookies.

"Mom must have despaired with the two of us. Me always twanging away on my guitar instead of learning how to cook a pot roast, and Kitaleen playing with her dolls and sewing doll clothes. When Mike married Kitaleen and they set up house in this trailer, he'd come home from working in the oil patch expecting to find steak and pie on the table and everything spic and span, and there would be Kitaleen sewing a party dress for one of her Barbies, two weeks' worth of laundry piled up all over the place, and not a thought in her head that it was even close to suppertime."

Too bad for Mike, I thought. My sympathies were entirely with my aunt and her dolls. As soon as I could handle a needle and a thread, she'd let me sew an evening cape for a Barbie she'd bought as a present for the baby that was due in a few weeks. Kitaleen was sure it would be a girl. The material, strung through with silver threads, had been left over from a show outfit Kitaleen had sewn for Gentry.

"Heavens to Betsy," Kitaleen said. "Aren't you the clever one. It's beautiful!"

Later that week, when Mike got home, he began yelling, plucking the glittery Barbie cape out of my fingers as I was tying it onto the doll.

"For Chrissake, what're you doin'?" he screamed at Kitaleen. "You wanna turn him into some kind of pansy?"

I remember wondering how playing with a Barbie might turn you into a flower.

Mike had a lot of words for me and even more for Kitaleen, and he used them often. I imagined on this Halloween he'd probably called her hippo or lardass before doing his big door-slam.

I sat down at the kitchen table next to her and helped myself to one of the toffees. I told her about the little boys and what Shon and his gang had done to them.

"Poor little tykes." Kitaleen shook her head. "Some

people just seem to have meanness bred into their bones. You have to wonder what makes them like that."

Three

The first day of junior high finally came. I had on new jeans that were only a bit dusty from the walk into town and a sweater that had been clean until three-year-old Lynetta coughed up her orange juice when I was feeding her. Most of the stain had come off by wiping with a wet facecloth. I wished I had new running shoes, but Gentry said her bank account was flatter than a Lethbridge farm field these days and we'd need to get things in stages.

Chantelle met me on the steps outside Mavis Buttley, and as we went into the school she hung onto my sleeve to steady herself. She had to guard against falling because her bones were so fragile, but I think maybe I was hanging onto her as much as she was hanging onto me.

Everyone who'd been in grade six at Acton Elementary was in the main hallway leading to the gym where we'd be assigned to home rooms. Shon and

Todd and Cameron were there, leaning into a bank of lockers and commenting as kids went by.

"Hey, freakface and fruitcake!" Shon said when he saw us. "Didja have a great summer?" Todd and Cameron whooped with laughter.

"Grow up," Chantelle muttered.

"Let's pray we don't get the same home room as those three," I whispered to Chantelle as we found chairs in the assembly.

Sometimes it doesn't help to pray.

We all ended up assigned to 7A. The only good thing was that Mr. Cambert was our home room teacher. He didn't put up with any guff from Shon and his gang but that didn't stop Shon from being his usual bully self when there weren't any teachers around. It hurt when Shon sideswiped me into an open locker or tripped me during gym, but I think the name-calling hurt even more. So many kids laughed, not just Todd and Cameron.

Shon had a pile of names he and his gang called me. It was Chantelle's idea for me to keep a list of them. Somehow writing them down made them less painful.

Sissy.

Crybaby.

Fruitfly.

Fagface.

Shon and Todd and Cameron didn't think to call me a fairy, though, until Chantelle and Amber Sadlowsky and I took on *Peter Pan* as a novel study project in grade seven.

Group work was Mr. Cambert's favorite way to fly. We hadn't been in grade seven for a month when he filled the blackboard with the titles of novels and had us sign up to do presentations. I wrote my name and Chantelle's beside *Peter Pan*.

When I was small, Gentry had given me a boxful of children's books she'd bought at a garage sale. *Peter Pan* had been my favorite. Of course it wasn't the whole big novel, just a little picture book with Walt Disney illustrations. But even back when I was only seven, I liked the idea of being able to fly off to Neverland.

"Good for you. Up for a challenge," Mr. Cambert said as he recorded the projects in his marking book. "Maybe Amber could go in with the two of you."

Amber Sadlowsky was one of those shy kids who always kept her desk tidy and hardly ever said two words to anyone. She'd come in late from a dentist appointment and had gone as pale as chalk when she saw the board full of names. She seemed happy when Mr. Cambert's suggestion got her in a group without any fuss.

"Of course the first thing you need to do is read

the novel. Carefully," Mr. Cambert told the class. "And then I want you to think of a special way to represent your ideas about the book. Could be a power-point presentation. A diorama. A skit or a puppet play."

Chantelle looked over at me and grinned. I'd shown her some of the puppets I'd been making over the years.

To start I'd had a toy box filled with hand puppets and three or four G.I. Joes. They had costumes I'd made out of Gentry's old neckerchiefs and other bits and pieces of silk and glitter from Kitaleen's sewing room. Barbie's cape had been just a beginning. In no time I'd begun piecing together outfits for the toys and putting them in little plays that unfolded on the stage of my green corduroy bedspread.

One of the G.I. Joes became a character called Spikehead, and he did have a wonderful headpiece I'd made out of half an earmuff and a plastic stiletto heel off a shoe Gentry had thrown into the garbage. Spikehead was self-centered and evil and yelled a lot.

My Red Riding Hood puppet, transformed into the movie star Medeena by gluing sequins all over her basic red outfit, was often the object of his wrath. Medeena was pretty good at holding her own against Spikehead. "Listen, heelbrain," she would shout at him. "Tell someone who gives a care."

Other characters were Prince Valance (another

G.I. Joe), Belladella, a sweet-natured Barbie with a broken leg who hid her handicap with long skirts, and Nosewart, the Red Riding Hood wolf who liked to wear hats decorated with partridge and prairie chicken feathers.

By the time Chantelle and Amber Sadlowsky came over so we could work on the puppet production of *Peter Pan*, my collection had grown to twenty-six. About half of these I'd made from used toys and odds and ends I'd found at the Goodwill store. In my mind, I had already cast the presentation. Nosewart would trade his hat for a lacy housemaid's cap to become Nana. A headband and a feather could turn Medeena into Tiger Lily.

Amber, who lived in a large new house with bay windows and gables and a three-car garage, looked a little unsure about entering Kitaleen's trailer. I was used to it but I could see why she was staring up at the second floor.

Our trailer was actually two trailers, one on top of the other. When Gentry made the deal for Kitaleen to look after me while she was on the road, they moved Gentry's trailer over from the other side of the court. Mike hired a crane and they hoisted Gentry's on top of the one they lived in. He cut a hole in the middle and built a steep stairway.

The bottom trailer was silver-colored and the top

was a kind of metallic turquoise. The strip Mike had applied seaming the two together was covered with pink plastic siding that was supposed to look like painted boards. The scaffolding to keep the upper story from collapsing in on the bottom had never been painted. Mike put in supports to create a verandah, but over the years the porch had become a storage area for a fridge and stove that had quit working, odds and ends of machinery he brought home and cardboard boxes filled with old clothing and junk.

It was definitely an odd-looking house.

I didn't often bring kids home. But I told Kitaleen ahead of time, and she took the hint and hid all the dirty laundry away. The dishes were done. Lynetta and Jasmine were having a nap, and the boys, Ashley and Holman, were doing their homework at the table over a tray of Graham crackers and melted marshmallows. Kitaleen's blonde curls were bouncy and shiny, and she was wearing a full muumuu-style dress. I had my eye on the leftover cloth for a party dress for Mrs. Darling in our play.

"Oh, wow!" Amber gulped when I opened the doors of what had once been the trailer's kitchen cupboards, but were now part of my upstairs bedroom. I used the bottom cabinet shelves and drawers for my clothes, but the top cabinets were for my puppets. I'd attached loops to them, catching the loops on cup hooks to start with and then screwing in wall hooks as my collection grew.

"Twenty-six," I said, a little breathless from our scramble up the stairs.

"Hey," Chantelle whispered. "Puppet king!"

Four

_____

Mr. Cambert helped us build a puppet stage.

"I've been meaning to do this for years," he said. "Every classroom should have a puppet stage."

We painted the plywood dark blue, and Amber made a design of different-sized stars that she filled in with gold sparkle glitter from a kit her grandmother had given her. Kitaleen sewed us some theater curtains out of her velvet grade-nine graduation gown.

The group presentations on novels took a week. On Monday four girls gave their version of *The Wizard of Oz*. They sang three songs from the movie. Melanie Ozipko had been taking voice lessons since she was in kindergarten. She sang "Somewhere Over the Rainbow" in a high, quavery voice to a tape of her music teacher's piano accompaniment. The other girls stood behind her and hummed, except for one song when each of them sang a line ending with "If I only had a heart" or "If I only had a brain."

As Joyce Jenkins tried to sing the brain part, Shon

Docker whispered loudly to Todd, "She ain't got a hope." Mr. Cambert aimed a look at him.

Another group of five did a skit based on *Anne of Green Gables*. This time Shon stuck a finger toward his open mouth as if he were going to throw up. Mr. Cambert pointed toward the door and he scuffed out of the room to sit on a bench just outside.

"This is a wonderful beginning to our week of novel celebrations," Mr. Cambert said as he perched on his desk. "I like the fact that people are doing different things. There'll be no homework at all this week so everybody can fine-tune their presentations. The groups that have presented theirs can turn their minds to mush watching television."

Chantelle slipped me a note.

We need to be better than what we saw today, so let's meet and practice.

We did. Every afternoon that week. Kitaleen stuffed the laundry into a little storage room, and she must have used up four bags of marshmallows for snacks that she brought up to my room where we were "fine-tuning."

Amber and I had trouble keeping from laughing when Chantelle did her lines for Tinker Bell. The voice seemed to be spun out of air and light. It was the voice of a child and a cranky old woman at the same time.

On Tuesday there were two more presentations. Kevin Albertson used his camcorder to make a video of the tripod invaders from *The White Mountains*. The tripods had been made out of Lego. You could see Kevin's and his cousin Roy's hands moving them around through the juniper bushes in the Albertsons' back yard. Blair Remple read a couple of pages from the book onto the video soundtrack. For sound effects, there were little beeps from Mrs. Albertson's stove timer.

Chantelle rolled her eyes and passed me a note that said, *Attack of the killer Lego!*

The next presentation, *Dragonwings*, was better, but Mr. Cambert had given Joey Gamlin and Spam Fordheimer a lot of help finding information on the internet about Chinatown and the San Francisco earthquake for their PowerPoint show. Spam's dad helped Spam make a model of *Dragonwings*, the airplane a Chinese laborer invented, and Spam passed it around the class.

On Wednesday it was Shon Docker's turn and, of course, Todd and Cameron were in his group. They did a scene from a Goosebumps book. Shon wore a blue fright wig, fake Dracula teeth, and had ketchup spattered down his shirt to look like blood. The presentation was good for about one and a half minutes but it went on for forty-five.

This time, I passed Chantelle a note.

It said, *Yawn*.

Amber had a Ukrainian Culture class to go to after school, so Chantelle and I went over lines by ourselves. When we'd finished, I asked Kitaleen if I could walk Chantelle home. I knew it was a long, slow walk for her.

When we got to edge of town with the hospital parking lot on one side of the street and Gumley's field on the other, Chantelle stumbled and fell. She just lay there for a moment in the ditch, not moving, like a small wounded animal.

"Let me help – " I knelt beside her.

Her face was twisted, as if she were crying, but there were no tears, no sound.

"I hate this," she whispered finally.

"What?"

"Everything. Being a freak."

"You're not – "

"A freak," Chantelle repeated. "It's not fair."

"Let me help you – "

"No," she said, struggling to her feet. For a couple of seconds I thought she was going to topple over again.

"I don't think you're a freak," I said.

"You don't count," she grumbled.

"What do you mean, I don't count?" I said, breaking the silence.

"You don't count because you're my friend."

The next afternoon, Megan Williams and Emma Lawton showed a diorama they'd made for *Sarah, Plain and Tall*. It had a farmhouse and a barn made out of Popsicle sticks, and they'd glued on some real dead grass, but they should have cut the grass shorter. It came up over the tops of the windows. They'd painted the outside of the diorama – a shoebox – pink, but the Hush Puppy lettering still showed through.

Their presentation, apart from the diorama, consisted of two words: "Any questions?"

Then six kids did a skit about Harriet the Spy. It was the best presentation yet. Malcolm McTavish played Sport and his cousin Alison McTavish played Harriet. Malcolm and Alison had always been the most popular kids in my grade, right from kindergarten up. There were many times when I wished I was Malcolm, with his perfectly gelled hair, his deepset green eyes and dark eyelashes, his clothes with expensive brand names showing.

After the shoebox version of *Sarah, Plain and Tall*, Mr. Cambert practically did a dance when Malcolm's group finished their skit. He said, "Great work, guys!" really loudly over everybody's clapping. Alison McTavish pushed her fake black-rimmed glasses down on her nose, chewed on her lip and began writing in her notebook just as if she were Harriet making notes about Mr. Cambert and the class. Everyone laughed and clapped again.

When Amber, Chantelle and I got back to my place, we did a dress rehearsal for Kitaleen and the kids. Kitaleen had even spent part of the afternoon making a practice stage out of an old refrigerator box. We pulled the drapes so it was dark in the living room and used a couple of Mike's heavy-duty flashlights for spotlights.

Throughout the play, my cousins Ashley and Holman sat wide-eyed in front of the stage. Ashley was in grade three and Holman in grade four, and the two of them had practically worn out my old Walt Disney book of *Peter Pan*. They knew the story inside out.

Kitaleen held Lynetta while five-year-old Jasmine wandered around the room. Even Jasmine, though, stopped and stood motionless when Tinker Bell twinkled across the stage on Chantelle's small hand.

Miserable Mike banged into the kitchen just as Chantelle was finishing her last scene.

"I thought maybe you'd surprise me, Kitaleen," he shouted from the kitchen doorway. "Thought maybe there'd be the smell of food cooking. What's going on anyway?"

I could see, through the refrigerator box opening, Kitaleen hoisting Lynetta onto her hip and hurrying out to the kitchen.

"Pipe down," she said in a loud whisper. "Travis has his friends here and they're working on a school project..."

In a minute Mike filled the doorway into the living room. "Things sure have changed since I went to school," he announced loudly. "We didn't have no dollies dancing around in cardboard boxes."

"Shut up and go get cleaned up," Kitaleen hissed. Lynetta began to whimper.

"We did stuff called arithmetic..."

"Butt out." Kitaleen poked him with her free hand.

"I think everything'll be fine for tomorrow," Chantelle whispered to me. "We almost got right through it."

Amber was already looking for her coat.

"We did spelling and geography..." Mike wasn't about to be pushed aside. "Hey, hi there, Amber. Say hi to your daddy from me. Your daddy and me did a science project together once."

"Nobody cares what you did." Kitaleen had put Lynetta down and she'd begun to howl.

"Of course, school was different back then."

"All of you were great," Kitaleen said as Chantelle did her little dip-and-dive walk across the kitchen where her jacket hung on a peg by the door. "Tinker Bell's going to bring down the house, Chantelle."

"I'll bring down the house if you don't get some supper going, Kitaleen." Mike dropped into one of the kitchen chairs and stared with disgust at the one plate on the table offering half a Graham cracker with melted marshmallow on top.

He waited until Amber and Chantelle were gone, though, before he really let loose. Mike liked to holler as loud as he could. I think it gave him a feeling of power to be able to fill a room with noise.

"Shut that baby up!" he shouted.

"She wouldn't be crying if you weren't hollering." Kitaleen was banging pots on the stove. "I thought you weren't coming home until late tonight."

"You hope."

I began packing the puppets back into one of Gentry's old suitcases so they'd be ready to take to school the next day.

"Travis, leave them dollies alone and get in here and help with things."

"Don't go picking on him now."

They were into a full round, I could see. I picked Lynetta up and headed to my room. The other kids trailed behind. Lynetta settled down when I gave her the Granny hand puppet to play with from my old Red Riding Hood set. Holman, Ashley and Jasmine sprawled on the bed while I did an updated version of *The Three Little Pigs* for them.

"Come on down. It's ready," Kitaleen called up the stairs about half an hour later. Mike was shoveling hamburger hash into his mouth as we filed to the table.

"You know, Travis," he muttered, "you keep doing school projects with the girls and playing with dollies and people are going to think you're some kind of three-dollar bill." He washed his mouthful of hamburger hash down with a beer. "God, Kitaleen, I don't know what you do to hamburger but it should probably be taken out to the back yard and buried."

I could see Kitaleen had been crying, and one side of her face was redder than the other. She didn't say anything.

After Mike finished eating and headed down to the bowling alley, I helped Kitaleen with the dishes.

"Don't pay him no mind," she said. "Ignorance is like a disease. Some people acquire it and it doesn't ever go away. There are times when it hardly shows, and times when it flares up and takes over."

"I want to tell Gentry," I said.

"What?"

"Tell her he's been hitting you again."

Kitaleen paused, and I could see the tears welling in her eyes. "No, sweetie," she said. "I just need to learn not to flare up like a grassfire in an August wind. I always tell you 'sticks and stones' and then I don't take my own advice." Water trickled from a dishrag in her hand onto the linoleum. "Your grandma always said the hardest advice for anyone to swallow is their own and I guess she was right."

When the children had been put to bed, Kitaleen sank into the living-room sofa. "Show me that part where the kids' dad is in the doghouse," she sighed. "It seems like such a good idea."

Our performance of *Peter Pan* took an hour. We were the last presentation and Mr. Cambert set aside most of the afternoon for us.

With the blinds pulled down, the tape recorder playing tinkly music-box piano, I came to know the wonderful feeling of power, of control, that comes from performance. For the first time I realized what it was that kept Gentry hopping from one dance spot to another. From Peter Pan's first appearance in the London nursery to the children's return at the end of the story, we pulled twenty-five grade sevens and one teacher with us to Neverland.

I used a high-pitched sputtery voice for Captain Hook. Everyone in the room laughed, and the laughter was like whatever magic lifted Peter and Wendy and sent them sailing over the towers of London.

Amber and Chantelle were caught up in it as well. In addition to playing Tinker Bell, Chantelle had a crocodile snout made out of papier mâché that fit over one hand. This was the crocodile that followed Captain Hook around, but was always given away by the ticking of a clock it had swallowed. Chantelle had the tick-tick-tick noise down pat.

When Tinker Bell drank Peter's poisoned medicine and began to die, it was only Shon Docker and his friends who booed when the audience was asked to clap if they believed in fairies.

When the play was finished, Mr. Cambert looked like he'd been struck on the head with a big Bugs Bunny hammer.

"I want to tell you," he said, "that this week has reminded me why I became a teacher."

The afternoon ended with a small party. Mr. Cambert provided the popcorn and juice.

When I went to pack the puppets at the end of our classes in the afternoon, Tinker Bell was missing.

"I hung her right up on the hook here," Chantelle insisted. "I don't mess with any of your puppets."

I found her on the way home. She'd been nailed to the trunk of an old poplar tree by the gate to the trailer park. Lots of nails so that it wouldn't be easy to pull her away. Also nailed to the tree was a scribbled note. It said:

Clap if you beleive all fairys should die.

Five

Chantelle and Amber and I all hoped that Mr. Cambert would be our language arts teacher right through junior high. But at the end of the school year, he took a teaching job in Edmonton.

"The siren call of the city," Gentry said. She was working on a song about how the cities were raiding country places. Mainly it had to do with farm boys giving up their daddies' fields for a life of trucking or warehouse work. But the boot seemed to fit Mr. Cambert, too.

On the final day of grade seven, Mr. Cambert filled in the challenge box he'd blocked off with colored chalk on one corner of the blackboard. Every week it had something different. One week it might be *Memorize "The Cremation of Sam McGee"*; another it would be *Guess the mystery author* and there'd be a bunch of clues about someone like Charles Dickens or Robert Louis Stevenson. If you met the challenge, you got free time on the computers on Friday afternoon.

His farewell challenge was *Read a book a week over the summer (yes, that's 8 books!)* or (this was in smaller print) *Read* A Midsummer Night's Dream *and turn it into a puppet play.*

Amber, Chantelle and I stayed after early dismissal that last day to help Mr. Cambert finish up his packing. As we cleared out the last of the cubbyholes and the mountain of taped boxes grew higher, I noticed he looked really tired and sad. I guess most teachers are tired at the end of June. And I knew in a way he was sorry to be leaving us.

"You wrote that for us, didn't you? That part about a puppet play of *A Midsummer Night's Dream*?"

"Of course," Mr. Cambert grinned. "And knowing you guys, you're not going to be able to get it out of your minds."

Chantelle uttered a little groan.

"You'll like it." He was looking straight at me. "It's spectacular. The king and queen of the fairies battling over a changeling child. While that's happening, a young woman, Hermia, is running away from home with her boyfriend, Lysander. Demetrius, who's supposed to marry Hermia, chases after them, and Helena, who's in love with Demetrius, chases after all of them."

"Sounds like my brothers and their girlfriends," Chantelle said.

For a couple of seconds the room was totally quiet except for a kamikaze fly on a mission against the empty aquarium. We were all looking at Chantelle. She blushed like she generally did when people looked at her.

"Well, you know. Wiley ran off with Latoya and she was Dwayne's girlfriend..."

"That's Shakespeare for you," Mr. Cambert chuckled. "A mirror held up to reality. But... " Mr. Cambert held up his pause-for-a-minute finger. "As if these stories weren't enough, Shakespeare plunks in a third – a bunch of amateur actors putting on a play, the Greek story of *Pyramus and Thisby*, for a bigwig wedding."

"Wow," I said. "We'll need a zillion puppets!"

"A few." Mr. Cambert checked his watch and got up to close the classroom windows. "I played Puck in a production we did when I was in grade eight. Puck's like the right-hand man – right-hand fairy, I guess – to Oberon the fairy king. Runs around with magic potions causing even more trouble. Needless to say," he added, clicking off the lights, "I was perfect for the part."

As he locked the door, I heard him mutter, "Wish I had a magic potion that'd whisk all these boxes to the city in the blink of an eye."

That summer, the first book Chantelle and I checked

out of the library was *A Midsummer Night's Dream.*
Actually it was a book about the size of a dictionary
called *Shakespeare's Comedies.* After we'd read a few
pages aloud, taking turns with the roles, Chantelle
looked at me and shook her head.

"I think Mr. Cambert was missing a few marbles
on this one," she said sadly. "It sounds like it was written in a foreign language."

We'd found our favorite spot in Buttley Park, a
bench tucked into some bushes on the far side of the
band shell. It was far enough away from the playground and the pool that there weren't kids running
all over the place. Kitaleen had given me an old beach
bag that had all kinds of compartments and pockets in
it to separate out sandwiches and sunscreen, magazines and notebooks. There was even room for a
gigantic beach towel with a picture of three body-
builders suntanning in Speedos.

Gentry, who was home for a few days, found it
when she was going through some boxes of things that
hadn't been opened since Grandma died.

"This towel," she told me, "was the envy of all my
girlfriends when I was fifteen. Everybody wanted to
have their picture taken lying on it. Lord, I think I've
got one of myself in a bikini lying right in the middle
between those two terrytowel studs."

I draped the open volume of *Shakespeare's*

Comedies over the chest of the body-builder in the polka-dot Speedo, so it looked like he'd fallen asleep reading it.

When Amber found us, I was stretched out on the towel next to the Shakespeare-reading body-builder with Chantelle on the other side of me.

Before we could stop her, Amber snapped a picture of us. She was never without her camera, which she carried around in a white canvas bag that matched the summery white and beige things of her wardrobe.

"Hey!" I screeched at her. "No fair!"

"If you only knew how you looked." Amber laughed and aimed the camera at us again.

Jumping up, I knocked over a jar of lemon Kool-Aid onto the towel-blanket. Chantelle twisted away from the flood, giving little Tinker Bell shrieks. By the time I'd chased Amber around the band shell and made her promise to hand over all prints when she had the film developed, Chantelle was doing what she could to save the Shakespeare, which had been drenched in Kool-Aid. She was patting the pages with a dry corner of the towel.

"So...are we going to do that play?" Amber asked when she'd caught her breath.

"Not unless we take pruning shears to it," Chantelle muttered.

"Long?"

"Long, and filled with withers and doths and speakest this and forsworn that..."

"I kind of liked parts of it," I said. "The stuff about fighting over the changeling child, and how he describes, you know, the spangled starlight."

Chantelle groaned.

"So who do I get to be?" Amber parked herself carefully on the bench where her eggshell-colored shorts would be safe from grass stains and spilled Kool-Aid.

"Still to be determined," I said, wondering myself where I'd got those words. "Hey, what time is it?"

Amber checked her watch, which had straps that could be changed to match whatever she happened to be wearing. Today it was a light beige. "Four thirty-three."

"Yikes! I'd better be going. I promised Kitaleen I'd pick up a couple of loaves of bread before supper."

We reloaded the beach bag, except for the towel which was still very damp.

"Here, you can wear it as a cape," Amber said, tying two corners under my chin so it hung down my back.

"Super Stud!" Chantelle and Amber both screamed and nearly killed themselves laughing.

I flounced the cape around. "Who could doubt it!"

They went with me to the Tom Boy to pick up the

bread. The cashier, Joey Gamlin's sister, who was a high school senior, looked at me as if a thirteen-year-old in a beefcake spectacular cape was just what you'd expect to see on a summer afternoon in an Acton grocery store.

That was when Mike's truck pulled up in front of the big window by the check-out counter. In two seconds he was in buying cigarettes.

"Hey, Mike," I said, my voice suddenly small and lost in the sound of the Tom Boy's fan. "Heading home?"

"Yeah," he growled. "Get in the truck." He tried to yank off the towel, but Amber's knot held and I began to choke so he let go.

"Get that thing off!" Mike said in a loud whisper. I could see Amber and Chantelle slinking away. I set the bread down and slipped it over my head.

"Godalmighty," Mike yelled as we headed out. "I can't believe you were parading around half naked with a bunch of beachboy pin-ups plastered on your back. And carrying a big purse! Don't you ever give a thought to what people'll say?"

He was still yelling at me when we got inside the trailer. Gentry, who'd been asleep when I'd left earlier that afternoon, gave Mike the eye.

"Give it a rest," she said. "I can't figure out what you're hollering about anyway."

"Well if you can't figure out what it means for a boy to be wearing male pin-ups..."

Kitaleen eased herself carefully down the steep staircase from the upper trailer.

"You all having a yelling contest?" she asked. She was wearing one of her shapeless summer muu-muus covered with Hawaiian hula dancers.

"I suppose because Kit's wearing girls in grass skirts, you think she's secretly in love with a troupe of Hawaiian dancing girls," Gentry said.

Kitaleen did a little mock hula dance.

"The only thing you'd attract doing that, Kitaleen, would be some lovesick hippopotamus." Mike made a noise like he was going to be sick.

"I guess you fit the bill yourself, Mike," Gentry said loudly.

At least Mike was sidetracked from thinking about Gentry's old beach towel. Even though it still wasn't dry, I quickly stuck it in a cupboard already bursting with dirty laundry.

"What's funny?" Holman said as he and the other kids tumbled into the kitchen. All of them were wearing shorts made out of the same material Kitaleen had used for her muu-muu. It was definitely the dancing troupe.

Gentry began laughing so hard she was nearly crying. Kitaleen started doing her hula again.

"God help us!" Mike roared. But even he couldn't keep from laughing, and Lynetta and Jasmine piled onto his lap.

All four of the kids went with me to the library the next day.

"It'll give Kitaleen and me a chance to do each other's hair," Gentry said, poking money into my pocket for snacks. "We ladies need some time to ourselves to get beautiful."

It took a long time to walk into town from the trailer court. Lynetta needed to be carried part of the way. Jasmine didn't need to be carried, but she was chubby and slow-moving, and she stopped for little rests at every large rock or tree stump. Ashley and Holman bounded back and forth across the road, checking under rocks for bugs and combing ditches for frogs.

They were all ready for snacks by the time we reached the hot dog stand across from the Buttley Park swimming pool where Chantelle met us. She was carrying the big volume of *Shakespeare's Comedies*. One corner of it was all swollen from its contact with the wave of lemon Kool-Aid.

When I explained to Miss Moberley, the librarian, about the accident, she looked at us sideways and said, "Some people find Shakespeare too dry to read but I have to say this is a unique way of addressing the problem."

In the kids' section of the library, Ashley found the books on spiders and kept running up to Chantelle to show her tarantulas and wolf spiders and brown recluses.

When Jasmine had been steered in the direction of the Curious George books, Chantelle and I began browsing through a section of fairy tales, myths and famous stories, where we found an illustrated retelling of *A Midsummer Night's Dream*. On its cover was a picture of Puck playing a long reed-like pipe, while very skinny fairies listened in the forest behind him.

"Anorexic," Chantelle noted. "I wonder what kind of a diet these fairies are on?"

"Nectar. Ambrosia."

"They could use some carbs."

Inside the book we found all the parts of the story that Mr. Cambert had mentioned to us. You could read it without feeling like you'd swallowed a dictionary of Old English. But even though it used actual phrases here and there from the play, I missed the longer stretches of poetry.

"We'll check this out," I decided, "but we need to renew the other one."

Miss Moberley sighed as she ran her scanner over these after she'd checked out the pile of books the kids had chosen. She stroked the water bulge on *Shakespeare's Comedies* like she was patting a wounded friend.

"Try to keep this away from the lemonade," she said, handing us the picture book.

"Come home with us, Chantelle," Jasmine begged. "You can read *Curious George* to me."

"Can't today." Chantelle brushed one of Jasmine's dark curls off her forehead. "I've got to keep an eye on Pop tonight."

We walked her to her place, and by the time we got back to the trailer park the kids were all tired and cranky. Lynetta curled up on Kitaleen's lap, her thumb in her mouth, while Gentry combed out Kitaleen's new perm.

"Hungry," Jasmine whined.

"Give her a slice of bread and some peanut butter, will you, Travis?" Kitaleen shifted Lynetta so she could look at her hair in a mirror.

"I don't know what possessed us to do hair on a day as hot as this," Gentry grumbled. "I can feel my curls wilting like week-old lettuce."

In the living room, Holman and Ashley had begun to scrap over a Nintendo game. They were into a full screaming match when Mike banged into the kitchen.

"What's going on?" he yelled. "Can't a man come home to a little peace and quiet?"

All of a sudden, it was quiet.

"God, it smells worse than an outhouse in here."

"Nothing stinkier than perm solution," Gentry agreed. "You're home early, aren't you?"

"Yeah, thought I'd check up and see what really happens here at home while I'm off earning a paycheck. Just like I figured. Kids acting up. Kitaleen wasting her time trying to make herself look good."

"Where you're concerned, it is a waste of time." Kitaleen gave herself a last check in the mirror. "Maybe you can look after the kids tonight and Gentry and me'll go into St. Paul dancing."

"Yeah, and maybe pigs'll fly right alongside you."

Jasmine burst out laughing, nearly choking on her bread and peanut butter. "Pigs can't fly!"

"And how come you're eating just an hour before supper?" Mike was working up to a roar. "Not that I see any supper being got ready."

Jasmine's laugh quickly changed into a sob.

"Leave her alone." Kitaleen put Lynetta down. "What's the matter? Everyone get sick of you at work?"

"In case you don't remember, I went in early this morning. You were snoring away so loud I'm surprised anyone in the whole house could sleep through it."

"Wasn't anything compared to the racket you made making yourself a cup of coffee." Gentry gave Jasmine a little hug and shooed her into the living room.

"I didn't see you getting up to help. You don't pay so much for board and babysitting it'd hurt you to lend a hand now and then."

"How much babysitting you been doing?" Gentry scooped the used boxes from the table into a plastic garbage bag. "Besides, I'd only been asleep for a couple of hours. Even when I'm not working, my body thinks it is and I never get to sleep before three. Needless to say, it was a delight to hear you crashing around at five-thirty. If I'd come down, I would've shot you."

I slipped into the living room. The boys had abandoned their Nintendo game and were watching a cartoon with the sound turned down to almost nothing.

The yelling in the kitchen rose and fell, and somewhere in the middle of it all, Gentry remembered a joke she'd heard and there was the sound of all the grownups laughing.

Holman and Ashley looked at me as if to say, "Can you figure this out?"

I shrugged and let the two little girls climb up on me in the La-Z-Boy. In a couple of seconds, Lynetta was asleep. I was half asleep myself. The story of *A Midsummer Night's Dream* was running through my mind, everything clearer as I thought about the illustrations in the picture book. The mixed-up young lovers. Bottom, the actor, given the head of a donkey by Puck, the mischievous fairy. Titania, the fairy queen, waking up and falling madly in love with Bottom – more of Puck's doing.

In the book, Puck said, "Lord, what fools these mortals be!"

To tell the truth, the grownups laughing and snorting in the kitchen sounded like they could have been part of the story.

As Mr. Cambert said, "That's Shakespeare – a mirror held up to reality."

Six

Chantelle and I worked on a puppet-play script for *A Midsummer Night's Dream* on and off for the rest of the summer. Amber had a Powerbook and she let us borrow it whenever we had a few pages ready to type in. By the time the first day of school rolled around again, we'd finished a draft.

The first chance we had to get into the computer lab with some free time, we e-mailed Mr. Cambert.

Am I surprised? he e-mailed back. *No. I knew you could do it. Hope you have a chance to actually put the play on. Right now, I need to plan a lesson for tomorrow. The school I'm at is "Academic" and it's a little scary looking at a bunch of grade eights who are probably smarter than I am. Wish me luck and good luck to the three of you.*

We ended up with another first-year teacher, Miss Eghart, for grade eight. Miss Eghart and Mr. Cambert were, as a line from one of Gentry's songs said, as "different as a country road and Jasper Avenue." Miss

Eghart liked a tidy classroom. All her desks were in rows. Everybody had the same book for reading. When we read novels from the school library, we filled out book-report sheets. Four for the year. If we read more, we didn't let on.

For a while Amber hung out with Chantelle and me. But then a couple of Alison's friends moved away, and Amber was suddenly going out for pizzas and off to movies with her. She'd still stop and chat, but mainly it was about what she was going to wear to Alison's birthday party or to a concert Alison's dad was taking them to in Edmonton.

One Saturday, as she breezed past the Goodwill store with Alison and Alison's friend, Jennifer White, she spied Chantelle and me in the racks by the window. For a second she looked as if she was going to pretend she didn't see us. But then she smiled and waved before turning her attention back to Alison and Jennifer.

"Sad," Chantelle commented. "It was good to have three of us. You know, more to fight the forces of evil."

"Yeah," I agreed. "But we're the awesome two. We'll just become awesomer."

"Yeah," said Chantelle. "That's us."

We were back on the prowl for puppet material. Chantelle was good at spotting hidden treasure. An appliqué of a sequined peacock on an old black crepe dress caught her attention. The peacock's glass eyes glinted at us.

"Titania?"

We said it at the same time.

The peacock would make a perfect cape for the fairy queen. I handed the dress to Chantelle. We always got a better bargain when she took things up to the counter.

"Tiny Tim ain't got nothin' on me," she whispered to me once when Mrs. Norshire practically gave her an old graduation dress with enough gold net on it to outfit the whole fairy troupe for *Midsummer*. She got the black crepe dress for next to nothing.

"Come over and we'll work on it," I said.

When Mr. Cambert left, he gave me the plywood puppet stage and Kitaleen let me set it up in one corner of the living room. It really bugged Miserable Mike, but, about some things, Kitaleen could be immovable.

"Travis does little shows for the kids," she told him. "It's a good way to keep them quiet while I get some of the chores done."

Mike snorted. "I don't see no chores getting done."

"Not surprising, Mike." Gentry was home for a few days. She sat at the kitchen table, smoking and nursing a coffee. "You got to be home longer than fifteen minutes to see chores getting done."

"Did I hear you giving advice about being at home, or is my hearing starting to go?" Mike tapped the palm of his hand against his head a couple of times.

"At least when I am home I give Kitaleen a hand with things. When was the last time you took the kids to the park?"

Although Gentry and Mike went at each other like cat and dog, I think Gentry kind of liked Mike. She would come home from whatever circuit she'd been on with a bunch of new bar-room jokes and make Mike laugh. It did make a change in him. I thought of Kitaleen telling me how he used to laugh more often.

Gentry would get Kitaleen laughing, too. "That's terrible, and you shouldn't use language like that in front of the children," Kitaleen would protest. "Jasmine seems to pick up bad words and chew on them like they were jelly beans."

It was Gentry who talked Mike into taking Kitaleen and the kids on a holiday to the mountains.

"My friend Arnie had a cancellation on a cabin," she told them, "and it's yours free for a week but you got to take it right away."

Mike generally took all of his holiday time in the fall to go hunting with his bowling buddies, so it was a surprise to everyone when he agreed. Kitaleen put her arms around him where he sat at the kitchen table and gave him a big hug, and then she was flying around the kitchen, running water into the washing machine, pulling kids' clothes and crumpled bedding out from where they'd been hidden at the backs of closets.

"Lord, Kit, slow down or you'll give yourself a heart attack," Gentry laughed.

When Gentry came up with this plan, it looked like she'd be home for that week at the end of June when I'd be writing my grade-eight finals. Then her agency called and said they had a gig for her at the Wagon Wheel Inn in Calgary.

"I hate to say no. Money's been scarcer round here than tits on a bullfrog," she said, pacing the living room. Chantelle and I were setting up the puppets for Cinderella to keep the children quiet while Kitaleen caught up on her ironing. "But, Lord, I don't like the thought of you being here by yourself."

"He can stay at my place," said a wispy Tinker Bell voice.

I had been in Chantelle's house only briefly and never beyond the front entrance in the years we'd been friends. At one time it had been a dormitory for high-school kids, back before the school bus routes were set up. The living room and kitchen were massive, and it made Chantelle seem smaller, somehow, than the cramped spaces of our trailer.

The building creaked like an old person trying to settle into a comfortable position. Chantelle said this was because years back when a wing had burned, some of the supports had been damaged. She showed me where part of a wall had recently caved in in what had been the boys' bedroom. Through the caved-in part we could see the tangle of charred wood, rusted bed springs and cabinets that had caught fire.

"Mama said it was Vern Saddler and Gordon Pyle smoking," Gentry told me. "Mom was cooking at the dormitory back then in the early fifties. She said those two were always up to no good. Likely drunk as skunks, too."

As I followed Chantelle up to the room I'd be using on the second floor, I could feel the initials and words carved into the banister. From Chantelle's father's bedroom came the sound of coughing and throat-clearing and loud nose-blowing.

Ed Boscombe, Kitaleen had told me, hadn't been well for years. "He hardly ever comes out of that bedroom, they say."

"Once in a while to yell at those boys when they're home raising hell," Gentry added. "Although, from what I've heard, he's not too sure half the time who they are."

When we passed by Ed Boscombe's room, the door was slightly open and a smell of stale cigarette smoke and something strong and medicinal came from the opening along with the coughing and snorting.

"Sounds like he's having a bad day," said Chantelle, lurching around a turn in the hall and pushing open the door to the room she and her mother had fixed up for me.

"This used to be Wiley's room," she said, "but there's not much chance of him coming home anytime soon." Although we'd never talked about it, I think she knew that I knew he was serving time in Fort Saskatchewan, a jail near Edmonton.

"Hey!" I said.

There were three framed pictures on the wall – sunbleached prints from the Disney cartoon version of *Peter Pan*. We'd looked at them in the Goodwill a few weeks ago. She must have gone back and bought them.

"Your bower," Chantelle said. For some time now we'd been sprinkling our conversation with words from *A Midsummer Night's Dream*.

We heard a clatter on the stairs, and in a minute Chantelle's mom was at the door.

"You're home, pumpkin." She patted Chantelle on the head. "Hi there, Travis. We're so glad Chantelle's having a friend over." Eva Boscombe was a small woman with a huge head of red hair.

"Mostly air," Gentry told me once. "If she teased it any more it'd start scrapping back."

She wore high-heeled open-toed pumps and a shiny pink dress.

"Now that her boys are grown up and mostly gone and Ed's best friends with his mattress, Eva thinks life is a party. At least she's always dressed like she's going to one." Gentry was intrigued with Eva Boscombe and had been trying to write a song about her.

"Any time Chantelle wants to have someone over, we're delighted," Eva said. "Aren't we, honeypie?" She patted Chantelle on the head again.

Chantelle cringed.

"Now you holler if you need anything. Chantelle, you show him where everything is." We watched her teeter back down the hall. Before she started down the stairs, she turned and called back, "Pizza for supper, you guys. I'm going out for a while. You like pizza, don't you, Travis?"

"Uh, sure," I told her. "My favorite."

Chantelle and I watched movies as we demolished a pepperoni, bacon and mushroom special from Metro's Pizza and Billiards. We watched *Peter Pan* first.

"Not as good as ours," Chantelle said.

"No way," I agreed.

Then we watched an old black-and-white version of *A Midsummer Night's Dream* that Chantelle had managed to tape by setting the VCR to grab it off the Arts channel at two in the morning. The young men, who didn't look so young, seemed to be wearing make-up and lipstick.

"Stage make-up," I said to Chantelle, as if I actually knew something about it. We loved Titania in her dress that looked like it had been spun out of Christmas tinsel, though. And Oberon in his dark cloak. When it came to the changeling child Titania and Oberon were fighting over, Chantelle rewound that part and watched it again.

"I think sometimes I'm a changeling," she said. "Left by accident, or by fairies making mischief."

"Me, too." I devoured the crust of the last piece of pizza.

"No, I'm serious." Chantelle looked at me the way she did every once in a while when she wanted to talk about something important.

"I mean... like a misfit. An accident," she added, as the lipsticked men chased girls through the woods.

I thought of the stories Gentry and Kitaleen had told me about Chantelle's birth.

"Do you think some accidents are on purpose?" she said.

I didn't know what to say. I wondered sometimes why Gentry had bothered having me. Why I was the way I was. Liking to play with puppets, liking to sew costumes for them and playing with them instead of playing hockey.

Maybe we were both changelings.

Seven

I had trouble going to sleep. I read for a while and when I did finally fall asleep, it seemed like I kept waking up. Once I heard Mr. Boscombe wheezing and coughing and Chantelle saying something to him, but I couldn't make it out. And then I thought I heard Mrs. Boscombe's high heels clattering along the hallway and her shushing someone who was with her. Then, in the darkest part of the night, I was wakened by the noise of motorcycle engines and loud voices beneath my window.

I looked out. Below me were Dwayne and Randy, two of the Boscombe boys, hooting and drinking beers and revving their Harleys. As I watched, a man slipped out a side door of the dorm and hurried across the street. Dwayne and Randy paused, their beers in mid-air.

"Hey, Penfield," Dwayne shouted, "good thing you're moving fast." He put his beer down, picked up a small rock and hucked it at the retreating figure. "It's hard to hit a moving target."

"Scat, you old tomcat," Randy hollered.

Chantelle's mom was out in the yard now, clutching her wrapper front.

"Hush," she said. "You're going to wake the whole neighborhood."

"Grab a brewski." Randy pulled a bottle away from a six-pack.

"I will, but come inside now before someone calls the cops."

I heard them tramp into the kitchen. There was a kind of whispered chatter alternating with loud bursts of talk. Then there was a rattling circle of sound from a dish or kettle dropped on the kitchen floor. A radio came on full blast before someone turned it down a bit, and I fell asleep to its low bass thumping. That and the rise and fall of voices and Ed Boscombe coughing and blowing his nose.

Chantelle and I were the only ones who got up before noon. The kitchen was littered with empty beer bottles and overflowing ashtrays.

"Looks like a good time was had by all," she commented. I began helping her clean up. "Did they keep you awake?"

"Only for a little while."

Chantelle made toast and coffee.

"It's what I always have for breakfast."

"Coffee?" Once in a while I had a cup – mostly milk and sugar – with Kitaleen.

It was an odd feeling, two fourteen-year-olds with our adult breakfast, alone in the big kitchen of the old dormitory. We sat at a table that must have served a dozen high school kids.

It was Sunday. We studied for the unit test in science the next day. Chantelle disliked the subject as much as I did, and we made up ridiculous sentences to help us memorize what we needed to know.

"Igneous rocks," Chantelle prompted.

"Please order bubble gum."

"Interpretation?"

"Pumice, obsidian, basalt, granite."

When we'd had enough science punishment, we pulled out the suitcase of puppets I'd brought and began practicing a scene from *A Midsummer Night's Dream*. Chantelle tried on the Puck I'd made from an old Smurf doll we'd bought at a garage sale. He was wearing leaves from an artificial flower arrangement Kitaleen had grown tired of.

On my hand, a straight-backed Oberon glittered with rhinestones embedded in black velvet and dark silk leaves.

We improvised most of our lines with a few words from Shakespeare here and there. But I'd memorized the words Oberon says to Puck in this part of the play, words like brocade threaded with silver and gold and pearls.

I know a bank where the wild thyme blows,
Where oxlips and the nodding violet grows,
Quite overcanopied with luscious woodbine,
With sweet musk roses, and with eglantine.
There sleeps Titania sometime of the night,
Lulled in these flowers with dances and delight;
And there the snake throws her enameled skin,
Weed wide enough to wrap a fairy in.

While we were in the midst of this, Randy stumbled downstairs.

"Hey, Chant," he muttered.

"Hey, Rando." Chantelle saluted him with a wave from Puck.

Randy looked like he was having trouble focusing.

"This is my buddy, Travis."

"Hey, Trav." Randy began searching his pockets for cigarettes, coming up empty-handed. A package on the TV stand was empty.

"Be a man's best friend," Randy said, more to me than to Chantelle. "Scoot over to Mrs. Harris's and bum a pack. Tell her I'll stop by later and pay her back. If I get me a smoke and I'm sure I'm going to live, I'll take you two on a ride later."

By the time we'd returned with Randy's cigarettes, Dwayne was up. He sat in an old armchair in the living room, a hand pressed to his forehead. He was naked except for his Levis, which looked like they might have been bought when he was a couple of sizes smaller. A tattooed eagle flapped its wings over his chest.

Chantelle introduced me to Dwayne.

"Howdy," Dwayne managed, although the word sounded like it caught on fuzz in his mouth.

Eva Boscombe straggled in from the kitchen. One side of her puffed-out hairdo had become squashed, giving her face a kind of lopsided look. Her coffee cup shook in her hand, spilling a little trail across the floor.

"Hiya, pumpkin," she said absently to Chantelle. "You kids enjoy your pizza and movies?" Easing herself into the other armchair, she added a few new coffee stains to upholstery already marked with a hundred splotches and cigarette burns. "Your dad's not very well this morning. Take him up a cup of tea. Maybe you could carry it, Travis."

Mr. Boscombe was in the middle of a coughing fit as we went into the room. His bed shook as he struggled to breathe, and it was a couple of minutes before he realized we were there.

"Chantelle?" His voice was quavery, as if he weren't quite sure who stood beside his bed.

"Tea, Pop?" she said. "You okay?"

"Dwayne?"

"No, this is my friend Travis. He's staying over for a few days."

I couldn't believe Mr. Boscombe had mistaken me for Dwayne, who was tall and weighed about two hundred pounds more than I did. And then I realized that for Mr. Boscombe, his boys were still my age.

Ed Boscombe sat up in bed to drink his tea. His eyes flickered back and forth between Chantelle and me as if he were trying to piece together some sort of puzzle.

"Ed Boscombe was an old man when he and Eva got married," I remembered Gentry telling me. "He must have been a bit fuzzy in the mind to marry her in the first place, and Lord knows he hasn't gotten any better over the years."

Mr. Boscombe began coughing again and the tea that was left did a little dance over his blankets. Chantelle captured the cup and set it down on the night stand.

"Eva," he gargled.

"I'll get her," Chantelle said and gestured for me to leave with her. Out in the hall, she stopped for a minute and rubbed fiercely at her eyes.

We went back to our puppet practice, and the afternoon wore on. With a steady supply of cigarettes and beer, the boys seemed to come to life. Dwayne even broke into a full-voice singalong with the radio.

"Hush," Eva scolded. "I think your dad's finally gone to sleep."

"Let's take these sprouts out for a spin." Randy was strutting around in his leather jacket, tossing his helmet up and down.

I had never been on a motorcycle. Randy put his helmet on me and went bareheaded himself.

"There won't be no cops where we're going," he said.

The helmet was too big and had a strange smell. Sweat and oil and dust and plastic. Mostly I smelled the leather of his jacket as I leaned my face into his back, my arms barely reaching around his middle.

Chantelle's face seemed to disappear under Dwayne's helmet.

We rode into a ridge of hills outside of town. A gravel company had taken bites here and there from the hills. Randy and Dwayne sped over the pocked landscape at a speed that left me breathless. Randy actually yelped at one point as my fingers slipped past the bottom of his jacket and dug into the flesh of his belly. Yelped, and then laughed.

I felt as if pain, injury and possibly death lay close and slippery like the gravel that tumbled along the gouged hills.

I heard Chantelle scream a high, wild cry like a hawk. Dwayne roared with laughter. It was a cool June afternoon with the rumble and ebb of the motorcycle engines somehow in tune with dark clouds scudding across the sky beyond the pines on the ridge. It rained as we made our way back into town.

Eva Boscombe had made supper while we were out, a steaming pot of chili put together from the contents of a countertop of opened tins. I was surprised to see Mr. Boscombe sitting at one end of the large table.

"Hey, Pop," Randy saluted him.

Mr. Boscombe stared at his son in puzzlement and then blew his nose loudly.

"Yo, Dad." Dwayne dropped into a chair beside the old man. Mr. Boscombe carefully picked the kidney beans out of his chili with a teaspoon, stopping every couple of minutes to blow his nose.

That evening we did the first part of *A Midsummer Night's Dream* for Dwayne, Randy and Eva. Ed Boscombe made his way slowly back to his room once dinner was finished. His coughing and nose-blowing came like the noise of a distant summer storm as we settled into the play. Eva fell asleep in her armchair, the puffy side of her hair against its back.

But Randy and Dwayne seemed drawn into the play.

"Fightin' over a kid, eh?" Dwayne said after

Chantelle had piped back at Oberon's demand for the changeling child: "Not for thy fairy kingdom!"

"Don't belong to neither one," said Randy.

Later, after Randy and Dwayne had headed over to visit a biker friend of theirs, Chantelle told me that Dwayne had a family and there was an ongoing fight over his two children – how often he should be allowed to see them – and his ex-wife's son from a previous relationship.

"Cody's always thought of Dwayne as his dad and now Tonya won't let Dwayne see him," Chantelle said. "She makes it as hard as possible for him to see Brad and Brianne. People can be so mean."

It was close to midnight when Randy and Dwayne came back to say goodbye before they began the long trip back to Hinton, where they both had afternoon shifts in the coal mine. I knew what Miserable Mike was like when he had a few beers under his belt and it was easy to see that Randy and Dwayne hadn't spent the evening drinking pop. But, while their voices had grown louder like Mike's, they were not edged with the same kind of meanness.

Randy squeezed my shoulder. "Hey, Trav," he said, "I'm glad you're a friend to Chant. You're a good friend, I can tell. She didn' have no friends before you."

"Oh, hush!" Chantelle turned red and pounded

her tiny fist into the arm of his leather jacket. "I've had a million friends. I just haven't told you guys. You'd scare them off."

"You be nice to Trav. No hittin' on him," Dwayne laughed. In a minute they were gone, shouting good-byes over the motorcycles' unmuffled roar as they peeled onto the side street. We could hear the machines getting louder as they gained Main Street and headed out of town.

Eight

Over the summer there was a change in teaching staff at Mavis Buttley Junior High.

"Mrs. Blenheim is gonzo," Chantelle told me on a rainy August morning. "The school board asked her to retire."

We were holed up in the children's section of the library, whispering over a small pile of books on puppetry and theatrical productions.

The home ec teacher had been striking fear into the hearts of kids for as long as anyone could remember.

"There is a God!" It was an expression I'd picked up from Gentry. "Who's taking her place?"

"I've seen her." Chantelle smiled. "She's nothing like the stitch-witch. She was buying a sweater at Toggle's and I heard her saying to Mrs. Petruk that she'd moved to Acton and would be teaching career and technology studies this year. Could be interesting."

"Yeah?"

"She looks like a movie star."

"Hey!" I said. "I'm going to sign up for fashion studies."

"I'd better sign up, too," Chantelle sighed. "To protect you. There'll be no one in the class but grade eight and nine girls, and that's pretty scary."

When I checked off fashion studies on my options sheet, though, I got called down to the school office. Mr. Stambaugh, the principal, held the paper at arm's length, as if his bifocals might be playing a trick on him.

"Fashion studies?" he said.

I nodded.

"We haven't had any boys signing up for this." He looked searchingly at me. "Now some of the guys have been putting down cooking. Food studies. It's something," – he stopped briefly and opened a desk drawer, as if the words he was looking for had fallen into it – "men are taking more interest in these days."

"But..."

"I like to do a bit of cooking myself, you know. Barbecue. Mrs. Stambaugh won't go near a barbecue."

"It's the sewing I'm interested in," I said. I was surprised to hear the words spilling out. "I don't want to do cooking. Or metal work."

"It's unusual," Mr. Stambaugh sighed. "What could have possessed you to take an interest in sewing? Do you know any men who sew?"

I didn't. "Mr. De Boer," I lied. "He's a tailor in St. Paul."

"I'm not sure tailoring is what Miss Riccio will be teaching. I think it's more how to make potholders and aprons…and such." Mr. Stambaugh put the pile of papers down and made a steeple roof with the fingers of his hands.

"Is there a rule I can't take fashion studies?" I asked. A flush crept onto Mr. Stambaugh's cheeks. It sounded like something Gentry would say. I remembered that last term there had been a challenge to the unwritten rule that girls weren't allowed to play hockey on the school team. The debate had ended with four girls joining the team, one of them getting more goals in the playoffs than any of the boys. "It's about time things changed," Gentry had said. "You'd think guys believed their jock straps were sacred vestments or something."

"No, it's not a rule," said Mr. Stambaugh. "Society has traditions, though…" He picked up my options sheet again and shook his head sadly. "If you want to be the only boy in a classful of girls making potholders, so be it, but don't come to me when the teasing begins."

A titter did run through the grade eight and nine girls when I walked into the home ec room for our first class. Miss Riccio was at the front of the room perched on her desk. She had blow-away red hair, bangle earrings and a big smile.

"Welcome everyone, and a special welcome to Travis," she said. "I'm hoping boys will soon be taking this course without any qualms but, at this point, you're the trailblazer."

Chantelle nudged me with her elbow.

"We live in an exciting world when it comes to fashion, body decoration, adornment," Miss Riccio said. "It's a world in which there are fewer and fewer limits on the expression of personal style. The thing is to be able to make good decisions about how to express, in fashion terms, what we want to say about ourselves."

She showed us a video of a recent fashion show. There were men modeling along with the women. A titter ran through the class again when three male models walked down the ramp in what looked like skirts. At the end of the ramp, one whipped his off to reveal shorts of the same fabric and then slung the skirt over his shoulders as a kind of poncho. Another sank into a lounging position and we could see the skirt was actually trousers. It looked like he was sitting in a balloon of Egyptian cotton. The third remained standing, but he flipped the bright red wrap back so it revealed bare legs and jack boots. There was a chorus of whistles.

Miss Riccio joined in the laughter. "Fashions are meant to be fun," she said when the video was over, "but before we're ready to begin strutting our stuff, we will need to learn some basics." She gave us all a handout called *Ready, Set, Sew.* "Look this over. It'll give you an idea of what we're covering in this course. You'll notice that ten percent of your mark is for reflecting thoughtfully on what you're doing. I want you to take the rest of the period and write a bit about yourself and what you hope this course will give you."

"Should I put down that what it mainly gives me is an escape from Mr. Foss's business module?" Chantelle whispered.

"Sure," I mumbled. But I was scribbling furiously.

When we met for the next class, Miss Riccio grouped me with those who'd taken Mrs. Blenheim's sewing option last term. "You know your basics," she said, "so we'll get you right into some project work."

As I reported to the other side of the room, Chantelle waved as if I were a soldier leaving for a tour in Croatia.

"Can you stay behind for a few minutes?" Miss Riccio said when the bell rang for lunch.

"Uh, sure," I said and quickly let Chantelle know she should go ahead to Metro's Pizza where we'd planned to meet for lunch.

Miss Riccio gestured for me to sit at one of the

tables. Sitting across from me, she smoothed back her tangle of curls and smiled.

"So, Travis…" She had the reflection sheet I'd filled out in front of her. "You've been sewing since you were eight years old. I expect you could probably teach the class yourself – how to use the sewing machine."

"Kitaleen, my aunt, she's got a pretty good one. She showed me how."

"You say you want to learn more about making costumes. Puppet costumes."

I stared at the green and beige mottled tiles of the home ec room floor. "It interests me," I murmured. I felt her hand on my sleeve.

"It interests me…" I could tell she was having fun with my way of saying things, but there was a kind of gentleness to it that made me look up, right into her eyes. "It interests me that it interests you. You say that it's a dream of yours to become a professional puppeteer."

"Yeah. You said to let you know how this course fits in with our dreams."

"I know." She had the kind of laughter that seemed to belong somewhere else, maybe at a party in some fancy city apartment, with people having cocktails, not a home ec room in Acton, population 872. A home ec room with water-stained drapes and arborite tables, their tops chipped away by bored students over the past twenty-five years. "I put that there just to see what kids would write. Thanks for surprising me. Did you know that professional puppeteers are like one in a million?"

"Not a big demand?" I said.

"No," she said, patting my arm again. "But sometimes you create the demand yourself. I think it's great, and I'm putting you on an individualized program. I think I might be able to show you a thing or two about the fine points of sewing. And drama. You lucked out, kid. Drama was my major for a while at university."

Chantelle had given up waiting for me and had pretty well finished her slice of pizza while the one she'd ordered for me grew cold. The restaurant buzzed with the noise of kids from Mavis Buttley and John Diefenbaker, the high school. The sound of billiard balls from the adjacent billiard room punctuated the racket, along with the outer space noise from video game machines along one wall.

"She said one in a million!" My voice skittered back and forth between highs and lows these days and came out as a little shriek as I filled Chantelle in on my talk with Miss Riccio.

"That's one too many."

The voice came from the booth behind.

I spun around. Todd Wingate and Shon Docker

were staring at me. I recognized the back of Cameron Coaldale's shaved head. Amber Sadlowsky was in the booth with them. She blushed and gave Shon a little hit on the arm.

Nine

– – – – – – – – – – – – – –

Amber began going out with Shon Docker the summer after grade eight.

"Someone must have dripped some magic potion on her," Chantelle concluded, "and she fell in love with a real donkey-head."

Chantelle saw Shon and Amber together once when she and her mother went to the movies and a couple of other times at the video arcade. During the summer, as we headed over to our hideaway by the band shell, we sometimes walked along the trail in Buttley Park leading to the swimming pool. We often saw Amber with Shon. When he wasn't sitting on the edge of the pool practicing curling his lip, he was showing off at the end of the high diving board. Sometimes Cameron Coaldale and Todd Wingate would be there, too, and they'd all be horsing around with the lifeguard giving them warnings.

"Amber's only fourteen and her dad says she's not allowed to date yet," Chantelle told me. "She's pretty good at sneaking out to see Shon, though. Must be hormone frenzy, I guess."

Although he had the personality of a rattlesnake, Chantelle and I did admit that Shon Docker had been in the right line-up when they were handing out looks. With each day of summer he turned a more intense shade of golden bronze. His ash blond hair was gelled to perfection. He even had abs and a slim waist.

"His mom takes him to the gym in St. Paul with her," Chantelle told me. Mrs. Docker worked as a cocktail waitress at the Acton Hotel. Gentry had told me that Benita Docker often said, "You look after your body and it'll look after you."

Seeing Amber sitting with him at Metro's gave me a funny feeling. Maybe it was the way Shon had her cornered in the booth, like she was his property. When she gave him that little hit on the arm, he grabbed her wrist and wouldn't let go.

"Give?" Shon grunted.

Amber didn't say anything.

Todd slurped his drink, burped loudly and said, "Better give."

What she did say then, very quietly, was "Shut up," and then, more loudly, "Ow! Stop it, Shon!"

"Give?"

"Okay, I give."

As we headed back to class, Chantelle told me that Amber had tears in her eyes and was rubbing her wrist.

"So what about our birthday party? Do we invite Amber?"

This was something we'd been talking about since the end of August. Chantelle's birthday was September 13th and mine was the 21st, and I'd convinced her we needed to celebrate on the Saturday between the two dates. We'd decided to have it at the dorm, but we couldn't decide who to invite.

Amber was really our only close friend from school, but this whole thing with Shon made it hard to figure out what to do.

"Let's just invite Amber and not say anything about Shon," Chantelle suggested. "But she may not come. I have a feeling Shon makes her check out everything she's doing with him. I hardly ever see her with Alison and Jennifer any more."

"Do you realize that so far that makes a party with just you and me and maybe your mom? Maybe your dad?"

"We could invite more kids from school." The way she said it I could tell she didn't want to. "You know who I'd really like to invite?"

"Who?"

"Kitaleen. And Ashley and Holman and Jasmine and Lynetta."

"Really?"

I was looking at Chantelle wide-eyed. She could still surprise me.

When I asked Kitaleen if she and the kids would like to come, she got more excited than I'd seen her in a long time.

"Let me make the cake." She began rummaging through a shelf where she kept her cookbooks. "How about this one?"

She showed me a page with a picture of a beautifully frosted cake on a silver platter. The top was covered with pastel-colored icing roses and matching candles. There was a bouquet of real roses in a crystal vase beside the cake.

"Looks great," I agreed.

Kitaleen's cake didn't look quite like the cake in the picture, but it wasn't bad. The layers hadn't baked evenly so it was a little lopsided, a problem she corrected with extra frosting on the dip-down edge. She put it on a nice serving plate that had belonged to Grandma – something called cranberry crystal.

Lynetta and Jasmine had helped mix the little bowls of colored icing for the roses.

"Honey, if you do any more finger-licking there won't be any left for the cake," Kitaleen said to Jasmine, winking at me.

"Ooh," both of the girls crooned when we'd tucked in the last of the fifteen curly candles.

"Jeez," Mike said when he came in for coffee. "Never seen you go to that much trouble for my birthday."

"You start treating people nice, maybe they'd think of it," Kitaleen mumbled.

"Nice is a two-way street," Mike said, plunking himself down with his coffee at the table and lunging a finger toward one of the yellow roses.

Kitaleen and the little girls all screamed at the same time. Mike's finger made the arc from the cake to his mouth with something like the speed of light. He made some loud smacking noises, but I could see he hadn't really touched the icing at all.

"Why do you always have to ruin things?" Kitaleen yelled.

"Didn't see no invitation for me." Mike made his voice a notch louder than Kitaleen's. "So I thought I'd better have my taste." Mike swiped the bowl with the yellow icing in it from Lynetta and ran his finger along the inside. Lynetta's howl filled the trailer and brought Holman and Ashley running in from the yard.

"Oh, pipe down," Mike hollered. "I was just getting a little taste. Seems like no one thinks about anyone but themselves around here. There's still some left in the bowl." Lynetta's howling turned into little sobs as she got the bowl back into her hands.

"I suppose you won't be happy 'til you have every-one crying." Kitaleen moved the cake to the cupboard counter.

"See what we got for Chantelle!" Holman had an armful of branches from berry bushes bright with red and orange leaves.

Ashley clutched a bouquet of late-blooming wild asters. "We just need something to hold them," he said.

Mike rolled his eyes to the ceiling and drained his coffee, "That'd be what she's wanting, I'm sure. A weed patch."

Mike wouldn't stick around to drive us in so we walked. We made a small parade. Holman and Ashley took turns carrying their flowers and branches in a big plastic bucket Kitaleen had covered with burlap and tied with a sparkly bow. Lynetta and Jasmine carried bits of costume jewelry they'd gift-wrapped with tin foil and tied with more of the sparkling ribbon Kitaleen had on a roll in the sewing room. I carried the cake, very carefully, in a cardboard box salvaged from the porch where it had been used for storing baby clothes Lynetta had outgrown. Kitaleen carried the beach bag full of board games, packages of licorice and toffees, and her own gifts wrapped in red fabric and tied with the never-ending supply of sparkling ribbon.

Chantelle was alone when we got to the dorm,

although a distant honking let us know Ed Boscombe was upstairs in his bedroom.

"Mom's just gone to pick up some things at the store." She ushered us into the big front room.

"Heavens, I don't think I've been in here since Eva's boys were little and she had a Tupperware party." Kitaleen scanned the room. "And that was ages ago."

"I love this bouquet!" Chantelle exclaimed, and she showed the boys where to set it on the coffee table. "Wow! I feel like I'm outside in a fall field."

Through the window, we could see Chantelle's mom hurrying up the walk, her arms loaded with groceries. I opened the door and took them from her. I could see packages of pretzels and peanuts, tins of pop and coils of sausage peeking out as I took the bags to the kitchen counter.

"It's amazing how a Saturday can slip away on you." Eva Boscombe gave my arm a little squeeze. "Hope you don't mind if your gift isn't wrapped, Travis." She fished a little bottle of after-shave out of one of the bags.

"Of course I don't know if you're using this yet." She tucked a strand of puffy hair back into place. "But, as the Boy Scouts say, be prepared."

She reached into a pocket and pulled out Chantelle's gift. A little gold chain with her birthstone on it.

Opening gifts probably isn't what people do first at most birthday parties. But the boys' flowers and Eva's presents got things rolling and there was no stopping.

Chantelle immediately clipped on the feather earrings from Jasmine and a mint-colored plastic barrette from Lynetta that looked like it had little bubbles inside. Kitaleen had made fabric pencil holders for both Chantelle and me, along with three-ring binders she'd covered with matching cloth. My four cousins had pooled their piggy-bank money to get me a video of *Hook* from the previously viewed bin at the video shop next to the Goodwill.

"It was Holman's idea," said Kitaleen. "He saw it when we were getting some movies a couple of weeks ago, and he wanted to know if it was Captain Hook, you know, from *Peter Pan*. 'Darned if I know,' I said, but we read the box and sure enough…"

"Hey, Holman," I said, and gave him a high five. He gave me a gap-toothed smile and blushed.

"Me, too!" Ashley got his own high five. "It's from all of us."

Chantelle opened her gift from me. It was a couple of rhinestone brooches in the shapes of butterflies that I'd found at the Goodwill.

"Ooh, pwetty," Lynetta cooed.

Chantelle held them this way and that in the window light. "Gorgeous. And don't think you're going to get them away from me for Titania to wear."

"The thought hadn't entered my mind," I lied.

Chantelle's gift to me was a chocolate box full of little plastic bottles filled with sequins and beads. It was hard to believe what I was seeing – enough glitter and glass for fifty *Midsummer* puppets. I saw Chantelle exchange looks with Kitaleen. She must have got into one of Kitaleen's craft catalogs and sent away for them.

"Awesome," I said.

We'd just started a game of Monopoly when the doorbell rang and there was Amber. She had a couple of perfectly wrapped little gifts tied with gold ribbon.

"Hey!" Sometimes one word can cover a lot of territory, and Amber, Chantelle and I all said it at the same time.

"I can't stay too long," Amber said. "But, hey, happy birthday!" She handed us our gifts. They were CDs – Chopin for Chantelle, Tchaikovsky for me.

"Of course, I don't know anything about classical," Amber laughed. "So I just got ones that started with the same letters as your names."

"Dwayne's been promising to get a CD player for the house," Eva said.

Amber looked like someone who wished she could take a present back and get something else.

"Miss Riccio will let us play them at school."

Chantelle leaned Chopin against the flower bucket, and I put Tchaikovsky beside him.

Amber teamed up with Jasmine, and they had just landed on Park Place when we heard motorcycles in the yard, their engines roaring and then dying.

Eva hurried in from the kitchen, a bowl of snacks in each hand. "Surprise! Surprise!" she said in a kind of stage shout as Dwayne and Randy stomped in, beaming, shedding leather, slinging fiberglass helmets into a corner.

"There she is!" Randy's face was covered with a stubble of red whiskers. He looked like he was trying to figure out how to get to Chantelle through the maze of Monopoly players on the floor. Dwayne, grinning, managed to maneuver his motorcycle boots through the obstacle course without too much damage to the game board.

"You be careful with those hugs," Eva reminded them. "You don't want to crack Chantelle's bones even if it is her birthday."

"I think they stopped off at a few places along the way," Chantelle whispered to me as we settled back into the game, Dwayne partnered up with Ashley and Randy teamed with Holman. Lynetta couldn't resist running her hands up and down Randy's leather chaps.

"Hey, little bit, you better keep your eye on your

money." Randy shook a finger at her that sent her giggling back to Kitaleen. "I'll steal anything I can get my hands on."

"He ain't kidding." Dwayne took a can of Pepsi from Eva and looked at it as if it came from some faraway world. "Randy's got the stickiest fingers of anyone I ever seen."

With Park Place and Boardwalk loaded with hotels, Amber and Jasmine finally took over the whole board.

"Lord, I'm done in and broke," Kitaleen sighed. "What else is new!"

"Is it time for the birthday cake yet?" Jasmine had been making trips into the kitchen all afternoon to check on it.

"Birthday cake! Birthday cake!" Randy started a chant that all the little kids picked up on. Amber had her camera out.

I caught Chantelle's eye as everyone sang "Happy Birthday." Lynetta had climbed into Dwayne's lap and Holman and Ashley made bookends against Randy, who was trying to sneak a twenty-dollar bill onto each of the saucers of cake being passed to Chantelle and me.

"I gots a yellow wose," Lynetta announced as she was handed her piece.

Amber was suddenly very interested in her watch. It had a dark brownish-red strap today.

"Hey," she said. "I've got to be going."

As we said goodbye to her at the door, I noticed Shon waiting down the street by the hotel, huddled into his jacket, looking our way. When Amber got close to him, he turned and walked away and she followed him down the street, trying to catch up without running.

"The course of true love..." Chantelle muttered.

When we decided to pop *Hook* into the video player, Randy said, "Time for the golden oldies to take the party over to the hotel."

"You of drinking age yet?" Dwayne asked Kitaleen, laughing.

"I'm not sure. What is it these days?"

I watched in amazement as Kitaleen got her coat and, after hunting around in the beach bag, found her change purse. "You all be good and do what Travis and Chantelle tell you," she said to the kids sprawled in front of the TV. I couldn't ever remember Kitaleen going out for a drink without Mike.

We'd watched all of *Hook* and half of *Home Alone 2* when Kitaleen came back, Mike trailing behind her.

"Look who I ran into in the beer parlor," she laughed with a toss of her long blonde curls.

Mike didn't say anything. He was looking at Kitaleen like she was someone he really didn't know. He even helped Lynetta and Jasmine get their coats on and didn't get after them for whining about wanting to see the rest of the movie.

"You bring Holman and Ashley home as soon as you're through the movie," Kitaleen said.

She ducked her chin, arched her eyebrows and gave me a little secret smile.

Ten

– – – – – – – – – – – – – – –

Since Shon had started going out with Amber, I couldn't help feeling he was watching for ways to get me. In Mr. Johnson's woodworking option in grade eight, he'd done things like spilling sawdust down the back of my shirt, or gluing my shop notebook to the table with wood-bonding glue.

This term, the beginning of grade nine, we didn't have any classes together, but Shon found out about me being the only boy in the sewing class. He began taping things to my locker door – a sample package of sanitary napkins, panties he'd probably stolen from someone's clothesline. Sometimes I caught him staring at me through the window of the door of the home ec room.

"It's creepy," I told Chantelle. "I feel like I'm being stalked."

"Take it as flattery," she said. "Stalkers go after people they're fascinated with."

"Yeah, like the fascination a cat has for a mouse."

Chantelle and I even decided to steer clear of Metro's Pizza and Billiards. Miss Riccio had suggested I bring my lunch and work on my puppet costumes over the lunch hour in the home ec room, and she was happy to have Chantelle come along and help me or work on her own projects.

Then in the last week of the sewing option, Miss Riccio came up with the idea that the puppet play could become a co-project with her drama class's grad presentation.

"*A Midsummer Night's Dream* for grad?"

"Sure," Miss Riccio laughed. "We can still have the fashion show that I'm told Acton's had at every grade nine grad for the last fifty years. But let's make the whole affair even classier. I think Malcolm McTavish would like to work on the script with you. Make the language more current; work in a few songs."

"Malcolm?"

"Yes. I mentioned it to him. He said you did an awesome *Peter Pan* in grade seven."

"Malcolm McTavish?" I didn't think Malcolm McTavish had ever given me a passing thought in his entire life.

"He's very musical." Miss Riccio pushed a plateful of cheese and apple pieces toward Chantelle and me.

"Sure. That'd be great." I looked at Chantelle who was looking sadly at the patchwork tote bag she was working on. The fact was she had very little flare for sewing. "It beats doing spread sheets for Mr. Foss," she said, but laughed at the way one strap had ended up being quite a bit shorter than the other, and the way the edges of some of the patches were coming loose.

I began staying late in the home ec room, finishing a black velvet curtain for the puppet stage. I was appliquéing a pattern of leaves and stars and a crescent moon onto the velvet.

"It's really too beautiful to be a curtain," Miss Riccio said. "Once the production is finished, I think you should put it on a frame. You could probably sell it as a wall decoration."

Miss Riccio was in and out of the room as I worked on the curtain. I lost track of the time as I stitched silver sequins onto the crescent moon, securing each one with a small bead pearl.

A tapping on the window startled me. I could see Todd Wingate, Cameron Coaldale and Shon Docker peering in. Todd had his nose pressed up against the window, looking even more demented than usual. Behind him, Shon and Cameron were jumping up and down and laughing hysterically.

I could feel myself blushing. I wondered if I could pretend I hadn't seen them. It was already after five. Kitaleen never paid much attention to what time I arrived home, but Gentry was coming back from a road trip and Kitaleen had plans to make lasagna. I'd offered to make a salad and garlic toast to go with it.

"Just stay away from ignorant, stupid bullies," Kitaleen had often told me. It seemed like the wisest course now. Anxious as I was to get home, I decided there was no way I was heading out of the school with them waiting for me. The salad would have to wait. Knowing Kitaleen, she'd probably be late with the lasagna anyway.

Miss Riccio returned from the office.

"Spectacular," she said, looking at the moon I'd just completed. "You are truly incredible." She gave my arm a squeeze. The tapping at the window had stopped.

"I'm going to have to lock up now." Miss Riccio began packing up her books.

"I've got to get going, too," I said, hanging the curtain on some hooks we'd put up on the home ec room wall. "My mom's going to be home for supper."

"Great," Miss Riccio smiled at me. "You don't see a whole lot of your mom, do you?"

"No. But we're good friends. We always just pick up wherever we left off." I stole a quick glance at the outside windows. The three were gone.

"I'd like to meet her sometime."

"She's not really into Mozart and Shakespeare," I

said, slipping on my jacket and grabbing my back-pack.

"Do you think I'm a snob?" Miss Riccio punched me playfully. "I like a good two-step myself."

I waved after Miss Riccio as she headed down-town. With the coming of October, it was already get-ting dark. Just thinking about walking along the high-way out to the trailer park gave me a funny feeling in my stomach. I could imagine the three waiting for me somewhere along the way, maybe in the small grove of poplars and saskatoon bushes just past the Welcome to Acton sign.

There was another way to the trailer court, past Gumley's farm and through a wooded area behind the park. It wasn't a shortcut – more of a longcut – but I struck off through the ditch and across the ball dia-mond to get to Mr. Gumley's field.

A wind had come up, cutting against me as I hur-ried over the stubble. It was a relief to reach the shel-ter of the trees on the other side of the field. The wind ruffled the tops of the aspen and birch trees, but along the cow trail in the grove, everything was still.

Then, from behind a bunch of willow bushes, the three jumped out, blocking the cow path.

I thought about turning and running. But maybe something of Gentry's blood stirred, and I decided to keep going.

"Hey!" Todd hailed me. "Where you goin', Cinderella?"

"Home," I mumbled, trying to edge past them.

"Just a minute." Cameron grabbed hold of my jacket. "We have something for you."

"What?" My voice cracked.

"Something." Shon pulled a jar out of his pocket. "Something special for a fairy. Make you shine a bit more than you already do."

"I haven't done anything to you guys," I said. "Let me go."

"We will." Shon waved the jar in his hand. "But first we want to show you what we think of sissies."

"Faggots," Todd said venomously. "What we think of nellies like you."

I tried pulling away but he flung me to the ground and was sitting astride me with his hands pinning my arms to the ground.

"Let me go," I hollered, as angry with the tears that were welling in my eyes as anything else. "I haven't done anything—"

Todd had begun unbuckling my belt.

I writhed and kicked.

"Here, I'll hold his legs." Todd laughed. "You polish him up, Shon."

Shon finished undoing my jeans, pulling them down around my knees.

"Hey, guys," he said. "He's not wearing pink panties today." He snapped the band of my shorts and then I felt him yank those down, too.

"No!" I screamed.

Shon began rubbing something gooey on my body.

"Shoe polish." Cameron leaned in close to my face, spitting the words into my ear. "Black."

I quit struggling. Above me, past Cameron's leering face, I could see the tops of the poplars whipping one way and then back again in the wind.

I felt that somehow I'd left my body and hovered high up there, watching the scene below. The three boys finally pulling back, shrieking with laughter. The one boy lying on a bed of dead leaves and grass, exposed, a smearing of black like tar.

The boy doesn't move. It is as if he is dead. The three stand around for a few minutes, kicking leaves, passing a cigarette. One hurls the empty jar into the willows, and then they head off.

How long does the boy lie there before he pulls his clothing back into place? As he struggles to his feet, before he can get up completely, he is sick. Like a dog, he kicks leaves and twigs over the mess.

It takes a while to stop crying.

Eleven

— — — — — — — — — — — — — — —

"Hi, sweetie," Gentry called as I let myself in the back door. "Come and give your old lady a kiss."

"Have to wash up first," I said. "I fell in some mud on the way home." I dashed across the kitchen without looking at anyone.

In my room I grabbed a change of clothes and then headed back to the bathroom. Jasmine was sitting on top of the vanity, clipping bright earrings onto her ears.

"Lookit what Auntie Gentie brought me!" She smiled a big lipsticked smile at me.

"You scoot now, Jassy. I've got to get cleaned up."

She shook her head so the bells on her earrings made little tinkling sounds as she left.

I locked the door and began running the water in the tub. My clothes were smeared with shoe polish. Shon had done a pretty thorough job on my skin, too. When I saw all the black on my body, I remembered a story Miss Thwarpe read us back in grade two. The Tar

Baby. I imagined Shon's hands becoming stuck, his fingers gummed onto my skin. I tried to put the image out of my mind. Shon's hands unable to leave my body.

I was careful not to run very much water. Miserable Mike always listened whenever a tap was turned on. If you ran it for three minutes, he'd be pounding on the door.

Rub as I did with the soap, the shoe polish didn't want to come off, although some did, leaving black smears across the inside of the tub. I found a rag draped over the elbow of the pipe beneath the sink and used that. The rag came away black. I hid it under a pile of tissues in the garbage can.

"You get lost, honey?" Gentry tapped at the bathroom door. "Kitaleen's fussing about the lasagna getting cold."

"I'll be out in a minute. I need to make a salad," I hollered at the door.

"I made the salad," Gentry said. "Didn't want to tell you earlier in case it gave you too much of a shock. Didn't want you keeling over in the bathtub."

"Thanks." I pulled on clean underwear, a T-shirt and jeans. For the time being I hid my dirty clothes in a cupboard already half full of laundry.

"Nobody ever waited supper for me when I was your age," Mike grumbled as I took my place at the table. "Didn't get there on time, you'd be lucky if there was anything left."

"Sounds like pigs at a trough," Gentry observed.

"Who you calling pigs?" Mike roared.

"No one," Gentry countered. "I was just making a comparison. We songwriters live by our comparisons, you know."

"Can't we just be civilized and enjoy our lasagna?" Kitaleen asked. Despite Gentry and Mike's bickering, she was beaming. For a change, what she'd cooked had turned out. The lasagna wasn't running into pools on our plates. The cheese on the top was crusty and brown, not burned.

"Wasn't me started calling comparisons," Mike said. "I don't care if you're Reba McIntyre herself, that's name-calling no matter what handle you want to put on it."

"I apologize," Gentry said, "in the interest of family relations." She winked at me. "What kept you so long at school, sweetie pie?"

I explained about the puppet stage curtain for the grad show. But my mind was filled with the things that had happened on the way home. Every couple of minutes, a shudder would catch inside me.

"Hope you aren't coming down with a cold," Gentry said.

"I gots a cold." Jasmine demonstrated a loud sniffle, jangling her earrings.

"Me, too," said Holman. "Mrs. Field says we should be taking vitamins."

"Mrs. Field?" Mike paused with a forkful of lasagna halfway to his mouth. A string of mozzarella trailed from it like a hanging vine.

"She's the nurse at school," said Ashley, presenting a small, hacking cough of his own.

"She must be new." Mike had managed to get everything, including the hanging mozzarella, into his mouth. "Mrs. Ryerson didn't go butting into people's private lives."

"Mrs. Ryerson retired four years ago," Gentry said. "You should give Shirley Field credit for taking on the job."

"We were all taking vitamins up until just a while back." Kitaleen brought the baking dish with the last of the lasagna to the table. "Lord knows it's the last thing I remember when I'm going up and down the aisles at the Tom Boy—"

"Oh, spare us. We don't need no blow-by-blow account of you in the supermarket." Mike nodded and Kitaleen eased a giant-sized square of lasagna onto his plate.

"Tell us about how things are going at school, kiddo." Gentry jumped into the lull in the vitamin argument. "You haven't cut any body parts off with a saw. Least nothing that's exposed."

"I'm not taking shop this term."

Gentry gave me a question-mark look.

"Fashion studies," I mumbled, "and computers." Louder on the last part.

"Fashion?" Gentry lit a cigarette. "What they got you doing in that?"

"Oh, you know, sewing. Finding out styles and patterns and colors that look good on you–"

"Sewing!" The last of Mike's lasagna exploded from his mouth, some of it raining down on Lynetta, who started to cry.

"For God's sake..." Kitaleen reached for the dishrag on the counter and began dabbing Lynetta's T-shirt.

"You're taking sewing!" Mike's voice was rising like an autumn storm. "I thought I'd heard everything–"

"Actually I'm working on costumes for a puppet show."

"Sewing and dollies!"

"Give it a rest," Gentry said. "Why shouldn't he take sewing? They don't give courses in ten-pin bowling and truckstop cussing, or you could teach that one."

"What's wrong is boys don't do sewing."

"Tailors do," I countered.

Mike looked baffled.

"People that make men's suits," Kitaleen said.

She had Lynetta on her lap and had got her to quit crying.

"How many other boys are taking this fashion stuff?" Mike wasn't letting go.

"Well, none this term, but Miss Riccio—"

"There. It's like I said. God, I don't know how I'm going to hold my head up..."

Suddenly I was crying. The more I tried not to, the more my body seemed to give into it. Shudders turned into sobs that started at my toes and settled in a pool of pain across my forehead.

"It's nothing to cry about." Mike's voice had quieted down a bit.

"Oh, shut up," Gentry said, balancing her cigarette momentarily on the ash tray. "I guess it's important to have stupid people like you around, Mike, otherwise we wouldn't appreciate intelligence when we saw it."

I pushed myself away from the table and ran up to my room. The yelling downstairs, which I could hear even through my closed door, was rising to full pitch. A couple of the little kids added their own wailing to the din. The sound rose and then faded. A door slamming made me think Mike had done his usual thing of storming out.

There was a tapping on my door.

"Honey?" It was Gentry.

"Yeah?"

"You okay?"

"Yeah."

"Can I come in?"

"Mm."

She sat down on the edge of the bed. Reaching over, she brushed back the hair that had fallen over my forehead into my eyes. Her fingers felt light, like you can imagine the fingers of a blind person reading Braille.

"You mustn't mind Mike," she said. "He's pretty ignorant but we're educating him." Gentry's fingers and a soft voice she rarely used brought the tears back to my eyes.

"How come I'm different?" I said. "What made me different?"

"Lord, we're all different." Gentry lit a cigarette. "It's just that, for some people, it's important that everybody be square pegs in square holes. Even if you're a round peg."

"But I'm more different."

"You're more special." Looking for something to flick her ashes into, she seized a small vase I'd made out of a mayonnaise jar for a grade-six art project. It was covered with shellacked coils of crepe paper. "I don't know, honey," she said.

"Am I like my dad?"

I'd asked Gentry a few times about Val. There was a picture of the three of us – Val and Gentry wearing cowboy outfits, and myself, at age two, with a little cowboy hat and fringed vest. It was a snapshot I'd matted with construction paper and stuck in a little shiny frame that had belonged to Grandma.

Gentry snorted. "Well, you do have those long thin hands of his. Artist's hands. Let's just hope you didn't inherit his roving eye."

Kitaleen told me once that Val Trask was more handsome than sin. "You should've seen him on the violin when he was playing in your mom's band. Trouble was he mixed a lot of fiddling around in with his fiddle playing, and your ma tolerated that for about a year before she sent him packing."

Gentry didn't like to talk about him.

"When it comes to mistakes," she'd say, "keep your eyes off the rear-view mirror and concentrate on the road ahead."

Kitaleen called up from the bottom of the stairs. "Come on down, you two, and have some dessert. I made marshmallow-cherry surprise."

"Lord help us if Kitaleen ever runs out of marshmallows!" Gentry stood up and stretched as much as she could in my crowded room and stamped her feet to get, as she often said, her "circulation circulating."

"We're coming," she hollered back. "It's not

important where you get your genes from." She dropped her cigarette butt into my art-project jar. "What's important is you stitch your own brand onto them. And wear it with pride."

Twelve

With another bath, a new bar of soap and some scrubbing with one of Kitaleen's old bottle brushes, I was able to get the rest of the shoe polish off. My skin was red and raw in places. When I saw Chantelle at school, she knew right away that something had happened. It took her about five minutes to get it out of me, even though I'd promised myself I'd never tell a soul.

Chantelle had been around her brothers long enough to pick up some choice words and phrases, and she used them now to curse Shon Docker, Cameron Coaldale and Todd Wingate.

"You need to tell someone," she said.

"No. They'll just find other ways to get me."

"If you told Miss Riccio, she'd think of something."

"No. I don't want Miss Riccio to know."

"Why?"

I didn't have a reason I could put into words. I wanted Miss Riccio to be separate somehow. I wanted her to be a part of the world where there were no Shon Dockers. Besides, what could she do? The attack hadn't happened at school.

"I'll be okay," I said. "They'll get tired of teasing me. They have before."

"That's not teasing," Chantelle said. "That's abuse – a physical attack."

"Yeah...well." I avoided her eyes. "Hey, did you get the options you wanted?"

"Mm...Mr. Change-the-Subject," she said. "I got drama and so did you. I asked Miss Riccio."

We did a high five. "See? There are things in this world that work out. Of course I know you were trying to get into Ready, Set, Sew Again!"

Chantelle made a face. "Yeah, right. Tote Bag 2. That's all I'd need!"

One evening I went over to Chantelle's and helped her fix up her tote bag. Eva Boscombe, who had recently turned blonde, paced the large living room chain-smoking as we worked at the table. From time to time she shot a glance at the telephone.

"What're you and Travis making?" she asked as she made another circuit of the room.

"It's either a tea cozy or a hat for Travis," Chantelle said. "We can't decide."

"That's nice," Eva murmured, patting her on the head.

Somewhere in the upper story of the old dorm, Mr. Boscombe blew his nose. Three times in a row. I thought of what a foghorn might sound like coming from a distance over the sea.

Miss Riccio had been showing me different embroidery stitches. I began repairing the sad patchwork of Chantelle's tote bag with bright patterns in embroidery yarn.

"Like Miss Riccio is going to believe I did this." Chantelle jabbed at my arm. She'd decided to abandon the tote bag altogether and was reading our script of *A Midsummer Night's Dream*.

"She won't care," I said. "She knows you're totally hopeless and need all the help you can get."

The phone rang. Eva, who'd just settled into one of the armchairs, nearly broke her ankle getting out of it. "Oh, nothing," she said after a minute. "Just helping Chantelle put together a tea cozy."

Chantelle rolled her eyes. She began reading aloud part of the play script so we wouldn't be listening to the phone conversation. It was the part where Helena is convinced all love has become a mockery.

"I think this is a part where Malcolm may want to put in a song. Remember, he said he was already working on something called "How Can Love Go So Wrong?"

We'd talked with Malcolm and made a date to

meet him at his place after school later in the week. In the past couple of months it seemed to me he had gone from being a cute kid to a heart-throb teenager. Chantelle laughed when Melanie Ozipko walked right into her open locker door because she'd been so preoccupied watching Malcolm going down the hall.

I noticed that Chantelle, though, had talked her mother into giving her a new haircut and a tint with a bluish sheen that brought out the violet color in her eyes.

"I'm going out for a little while," Eva announced as she put the phone down. "You listen for your dad, honey. If he needs anything..."

Malcolm McTavish's father was Acton's doctor. The Acton Clinic was a block off Main Street in a red-brick building that stretched from the alley to the corner. On the day we agreed to meet, we followed him into the clinic, where his mom worked as a nurse receptionist.

"Hey, Mom." Malcolm adjusted his backpack to give her a kiss on the cheek.

"Hi, Mac," she said. Her smile was filled with perfect white teeth. "Mrs. Shebansky, you can go on in now." She nodded to an old woman wearing a baboushka.

"Ai-yi," Mrs. Shebansky said as she struggled out

of the waiting room chair and began hobbling across the room with the help of a cane. "This your boy?" she said when she got as far as the reception desk.

"Yes. We'll keep him until something better comes along," Mrs. McTavish laughed.

"He's a nice boy. I can see." Mrs. Shebansky continued her slow journey.

"Get the door for her, honey." Mrs. McTavish was smiling at Chantelle and me now. "Goodness, I think you're an inch taller every time I see you these days, Travis." She paused for a moment, the way people often did before greeting Chantelle. "What a lovely hairstyle, Chantelle!"

"Is it okay if I make nachos?" Malcolm was back.

"Sure, hon." Mrs. McTavish picked up a stack of files from her desk. "I think it's written in the teenage bill of rights somewhere that appetites for regular meals should be spoiled at every opportunity." She flashed us the smile again. "Your dad has to work late tonight anyway, so we'll all have a late supper."

Chantelle and I tried not to look at each other. Malcolm's mom talked like someone from a different world – a world of old TV shows like The Brady Bunch.

"C'mon." Malcolm led the way to the back door of the clinic and then through a yard with trimmed shrubs and lacy iron chairs and benches to the back door of the house.

"Throw your coats anywhere." He gestured at wicker lounges and chairs in the sun porch. Chantelle eased her backpack onto a glass-top table, careful not to disturb the *House and Garden* magazines laid out on it.

In the kitchen, Malcolm spilled nacho chips onto a platter. "You want to grate some cheese over this?" He handed me a block of Cheddar and a stainless-steel grater. "And I'll get us some drinks. What would you like, Chantelle?"

Chantelle just looked at him. It reminded me of the way she'd been during those first years of school when she hadn't talked at all.

"Coke?"

"Yeah. Sure." Her voice was tiny in the big room.

"Me, too," I said.

"Thanks," Chantelle added.

Copper pots that looked like they'd never been used hung from a rack attached to the ceiling. There was more copper in the jelly molds lining the walls above the cupboards. Dried straw flowers poked out of a huge basket at the end of the counter.

When the nachos were heated, Malcolm whisked the platter along with our Cokes onto a tray with handles, the kind people use in movies to serve breakfast to people in bed, and we followed him down the hall.

"We might as well work in my room," he said, "in case we want to play around with the music."

In Malcolm's room, Chantelle and I were stunned again into silence. The room seemed bigger than a whole floor of Kitaleen's trailer. Along one wall there were bookshelves – one had a TV tucked into it – and a desk set up with a computer. Beside that was an electronic keyboard and a sound system. Malcolm plunked the tray down on a table rising like an island out of a Navajo rug in the middle of the room.

"Pardon the mess," he said, waving an arm toward the other side of the room, its unmade bed and some clothes that hadn't been put away.

"As long as you don't let it happen again," Chantelle quipped. She was beginning to find her voice again.

"Yes, Mom." Malcolm bit into a nacho, letting the melted cheese dance across his fingers.

When we'd reduced the nachos to a few crumbs, Malcolm pulled a file out of a desk drawer.

"Let me show you what I've been thinking about."

I can't remember a whole lot of what Malcolm said as we sat around his table that afternoon. I heard the excitement in his voice, sentences that raced along, tripping at times on bits of laughter. An overhead light played across his hair, finding a coppery color here and there like the pots hanging in the kitchen. As he talked, Malcolm's hands made circles in the air to snare the point of something he'd said, fingers dancing up and down over an imaginary keyboard when he talked about the music.

"We keep in the parts that keep the story moving." He reached over and his hand lit briefly on my arm. I felt it like an electric current. "And, for the poetry, we use songs. I've done a couple already." In a minute he was at the keyboard and a slow recurring bass beat filled the room. Malcolm's fingers traced a melody pattern and he began singing:

Why was I
To this keen mockery born?
When – at your hands –
Did I deserve this scorn?
Why do I
*   deserve this scorn...*

"Do you want to try singing it, Chantelle?" He spun around. "You're going to do Helena, aren't you?"

"I don't sing," said Chantelle. "I'll do Puck and the fairies."

"With puppets," I said, "it doesn't matter who sings. We're all hidden behind the stage anyway."

"Or the music could be taped," Malcolm mused.

It's odd how the world can change in a day. I think both Chantelle and I realized that getting to know

Malcolm would make the pattern of what was to come different somehow. As I walked home, I kept looking up at the spattered sky. In a way, the stars seemed secure – as if they'd been stitched to the fabric of the night – and yet I half expected to see "certain stars shoot madly from their spheres," just the way Oberon does when he sends Puck to fetch the magic love potion.

Sure enough, I did see a falling star. I was so startled, I nearly tripped and fell into the ditch by the Welcome to Acton sign.

Thirteen

Midway into our second set of options, Miss Riccio and the music teacher, Mrs. Dahlbeck, called a meeting to begin planning the grad production.

Mrs. Dahlbeck worked part-time at the school. She also gave private piano lessons to people like Malcolm McTavish.

"I think she has a split personality," Malcolm told us the evening we were over at his house. "I call her Jekyll-Hyde Dahlbeck. After one of my lessons, she slammed the keyboard cover down so hard on her Steinway that it cracked the wood. Then she started screaming at me as if I'd done it. All I did was murder a little piece by Mozart."

Mrs. Dahlbeck was a plump, pale lady with hair that looked like it had been sprayed into place in the 1960s. "We need to know how many singers we have." She spoke with an accent, and "singers" came out as "zingers."

"And who will play some instruments. Zingers

first." There were seven girls – mainly friends of Melanie Ozipko – and one boy, the Anglican minister's son, Gregory, who joined all the school clubs because his mother made him.

In addition to Malcolm on the keyboard, there were only three for instruments. Malcolm's cousin Alison, who played the flute; Garnett Zdrill, who'd brought along his accordion; and Melanie Ozipko's sister Agnes, who wanted to know if she could play her cello.

"We will figure it out." Mrs. Dahlbeck smiled at us and nodded to Miss Riccio, who'd been waiting at the side.

"Wow." Miss Riccio exhaled the word to the accompaniment of a jangle of bracelets. "I can't tell you how excited I am about this project."

The thing about Miss Riccio was that she actually did look excited. Her cheeks were flushed. Her hair appeared more fiery than usual. She seemed to have put on extra jewelry for our meeting.

"There's an amazing amount of talent in this room, and I think, well, I think we're just going to knock the socks off–"

The door to the music-drama room flew open and Amber Sadlowsky, seeing the meeting was in progress, tiptoed to the back of the room and slipped into the seat beside Chantelle. She looked like she had been crying. I saw Chantelle's tiny hand reach over and heard her whisper, "Hey."

"Hey," Amber whispered back.

"...and this will be a work in progress," Miss Riccio was saying when I was finally able to pull my attention away from Amber and back to the meeting. "Travis and Chantelle will be fine-tuning the script. And Malcolm will be developing songs over the next three or four months. Once he's finished, Mrs. Dahlbeck will begin rehearsing it with the musicians. Amber, are you going to join the chorus?"

Amber looked startled. "Uh, no I'll help with the puppets," she said.

"Yes!" Chantelle said in a loud whisper.

About once a week, Malcolm had us over to his house to update us on the progress he was making on the music for the play. Amber began coming with us. She didn't want to talk about what had upset her the day she joined the drama club, although Chantelle was bending over backwards feeding her lead-in lines.

"I hope he hasn't been beating on her," Chantelle said to me. "You never know with people like Shon."

However Shon was treating her, Amber was still going out with him, was still known around Mavis Buttley as Shon's girl. On the days when she walked with us to or from school, if Shon appeared, she left us to join him.

Scheduling threw all of us into the same communication technologies class in the spring. Shon made sure Amber sat at the computer next to him. As for me, he seemed to be content with curling his lip or making retching noises when he happened to catch my eye while Mr. Foss was out of the room.

Part of our course included forwarding websites of interest to one another, and there were some days when Shon was focused enough to actually track down sites on feminine hygiene or gay porn and e-mail them to me. Most of the time I simply deleted them unopened, but he got cagier at finding sites that had the possibility of something to do with drama, puppetry or the Greek setting of *A Midsummer Night's Dream*. He'd even figured out a way to make it look as if the sites were forwarded from another computer.

When I mentioned this to Chantelle, she said, "The next time it happens, chuck a paper wad at me and I'll come over."

Mr. Foss was out of the room when it happened. He'd made his usual getaway for a coffee about fifteen minutes into the class after delivering a mini-lecture and setting an assignment. Chantelle had e-mailed me a site on Elizabethan theater and, I thought, one on Greek mythology. When I clicked on "The Greek

Way," though, a disclaimer came up saying visitors needed to be over eighteen. I chucked a paper wad at Chantelle and, in the process, knocked the mouse off my desk, sending it banging back and forth against the desk leg. Chantelle heard my "aaagh" as the screen exploded with nude men in the middle of Greek ruins.

"Hmm. I think Shon has secrets he wants to share," she announced, staring at my screen. "Or maybe Shon's picture is actually here somewhere."

"You wish," Shon snarled.

At that point, Mr. Foss came back into the room and saw my screen. He gasped. When he flung his arm out toward me, coffee went flying in a spectacular arc over the floor.

"Travis Trask!" His face was splotched with red and he was sputtering to find words. "Log out this minute!"

"But Mr. Foss..." Chantelle's high, thin voice found a space in Mr. Foss's rant. I shot her a look, though, and shook my head.

"What are you doing away from your station?" he shouted at Chantelle. "I was wrong, I see, to expect some maturity from grade nines." He looked sadly at his empty coffee cup. "Everyone get back to their assignments. And you, Mr. Trask, once you have deleted that site, and emptied your trash, will go to the library and stay there until I have a chance to talk with you. Did you hear me? Everyone back to work or there'll be a full class detention."

"But that's not fair—" Shon complained.

"Not one word out of you, Shon Docker, or you'll be cooling your heels in the library, too."

I tried to get out of the website, but it turned out to be one that pops you into another page as soon as you close it. In a panic I scooted the cursor to Shutdown.

Chantelle had gone slowly back to her own station. Malcolm, though, was half out of his desk, getting ready to go and see Mr. Foss. I got his attention and shook my head. He mouthed the word yes and nodded. But I shook my head no and gathered up my books.

As I was leaving, Amber looked up and gave me a little smile. Shon glared at her.

At break, both Malcolm and Chantelle hurried into the library before Mr. Foss got there.

"You're going to tell him," they said in chorus.

"Uh-uh," I said. "It just wouldn't be worth it."

"You can't let him keep on…" I'd never really seen Malcolm angry before. The animation that I'd noticed when he was telling us about his music or showing us something he was working on seemed to be at fast forward.

"See you at three-thirty," he said, but I could tell he didn't want to let it go.

It wasn't Malcolm and Chantelle I saw when the dismissal buzzer went, though. It was Mike, standing in the front foyer holding Lynetta. She was crying and looked like her eyes and nose had been streaming all afternoon. I had a feeling Mike wasn't waiting with glad tidings.

"Mike!" I said, trying to sound like I was happy to see him. "What's up?"

"What's up is Kitaleen's broke her leg," Mike grumbled, shifting Lynetta to his other side. "You're going to have to get right home. I'm on call this week."

"But I'm supposed to go over to Malcolm's—"

"Forget it," Mike snarled. "Get in the truck."

"What happened?" I said as Mike fishtailed away from the school.

"Fell downstairs." Mike was grim-faced. "I swear your aunt's the clumsiest person I ever seen in my life. And it don't help that she weighs as much as a loaded semi. All that weight coming down...no wonder the bones were cracked in more than one place."

I didn't say anything. But I felt like part of me was slipping, moving faster and faster down a steep, muddy slope.

"And I don't want to hear no guff from you." Mike

was starting to yell. "You're gonna have to get home right after school. Forget about all your dollies and play-acting."

Inside I was skidding faster down the hill, falling, out of control.

"Of course, it would be asking too much for your mother to show her face around here and help out a bit. For God's sake, Lynetta, quit bawling…"

I held Lynetta closer to me and patted her back. I was able to gasp for air a couple of times in sync with her.

Steadying. Going slower.

Fourteen

--- -- -- -- -- -- -- -- -- -- --

I got to know things about life in the double-decker trailer in those days just after Kitaleen broke her leg, when getting out of bed was such a struggle she sometimes stayed in her room all day. Things I'd never really paid attention to before. Like the kind of water we had which left brown rings in the tub and sinks that Comet couldn't take off no matter how much you scrubbed. And the washing machine dial that wouldn't click into hot, so loads of wet clothes were icy cold and the soap powder sometimes stayed in a solid lump like wet sand.

What else? If you forgot to take hamburger out of the freezer, you could spend a lot of time trying to get it to thaw out in a frying pan at supper time. The importance of checking that there was bread for sandwiches before eleven o'clock at night when the stores closed. If there wasn't any, you'd have to walk a mile to the truck stop that was open all night on the highway. You needed to watch that Jasmine didn't sneak chocolate, which she was allergic to, up to her room to eat when no one was looking. You needed to help Holman with his math homework, even if you weren't very good at it yourself.

When Gentry phoned to see how things were going and I told her what had happened, she gave a little yelp and said, "I knew that stupid stairway Mike built would do someone in one of these days. I've come close to breaking my ankle on it more 'n once." She went on to say that she wouldn't be able to get back to Acton for at least three weeks.

"Do what you can, honey, to help Kitaleen. Mike won't be no more use than a feather duster in a hayloft." I could hear a bit of a party going on in the background. "Hey, babe," someone asked loudly, "where'd you say them extra glasses was?"

"Hold your horses, Dwight," Gentry said just as loudly, and then more quietly to me, "I better go, sweetie. We got a guitar player now with a fuse shorter 'n a clump of grass in a cow pasture."

"Sure. See you in three weeks."

Kitaleen had a cast that started at her toes and went nearly up to her waist. The first few times she struggled to get from her bed to the living-room La-Z-Boy on crutches, she wept openly from the pain.

"Travis," she kept telling me, "I'm so sorry. In a few days I should be moving around better."

"We can help," Jasmine said, running her hands along the plaster cast as if that would somehow make her mother feel better.

The kids did try to help, but I still ended up doing most of the chores as well as getting them bathed and into bed at night. Mike's idea of helping was to sit at the supper table or in front of the TV and yell at them to do things.

What Kitaleen did, as some of her energy came back, was take over the sewing of the fairy puppets for *A Midsummer Night's Dream*. "That's the least I can do," she said when I pulled them out of a box late one evening. We'd decided to do the fairies as gloves with a small head on each finger and tiny tunics of the gold netting we'd found at the Goodwill. It was the first time since the accident that I'd seen Kitaleen sort of come to life. A bit of color found its way into her cheeks.

"I can't believe what I'm seeing," Miserable Mike said the first time he caught her working on them. "Can't you find nothing useful to do while you're parked in the La-Z-Boy?"

"Like what?"

"Like..." Mike sputtered. "Mending socks..."

Mike could find something to holler about before

he got his boot laces untied. If there was one stage direction for him, it would be "Enter yelling."

"I thought Kitaleen was the worst cook in the world," he complained one evening as I dished up a mixture of macaroni and hamburger. "Compared to you, Travis, she's Martha Stewart."

"I don't see you rushing home to help," Kitaleen said, hobbling from the living room on her crutches. "I think he's been doing more than his share–"

"Well, I don't see you bringing home no paycheck." Mike grabbed the ketchup bottle and shook about half of it over his supper.

"Slave labor don't get a paycheck." Kitaleen eased herself onto a chair placed sideways. "Ashley, honey, get me that kitchen stool. The doctor says to keep my leg elevated..."

"Slave labor! Ha!" Mike stirred the mess around on his plate with a fork he was holding like a piece of pipeline equipment. "If you ask me, you're living the life of the Queen of Sheba–"

"No one asked you."

I could see Holman and Jasmine exchanging looks. Lynetta began to whine.

"Ayaagh." Mike made a noise in his throat and sent his plate spinning across the table. "I can't eat this crap. I'm going over to Metro's for something that don't make me want to throw up."

"We're going to miss you," Kitaleen shouted after him as he pulled on his boots and parka. "Can't imagine who's going to give the kids their baths and get them into bed—"

"Aw, shut up!" He slammed the door as he went out.

"...and read them their bedtime stories," she added lamely.

Some days at school I was finding it hard to keep awake. I made Chantelle promise to poke me in the ribs if I nodded off in Mr. Stambaugh's science class, and Malcolm had the job during math. I did fall asleep in my chair as we began a new assignment in communication technologies. When I woke up, I saw Mr. Foss looking at me with concern over the rim of his coffee cup. I could read the printing on it: *Old teachers never die. They just lose their class.*

At lunch hour, Miss Riccio invited people from the drama club and choir to gather together in the home ec room. It became a little island in each schoolday — escape for an hour with a chance to go over lines, work on puppets and props, goof around a bit. Miss Riccio let people bring in their favorite CDs and play them as long as she was given equal time for Mozart and what she called the Big B guys: Bach, Beethoven and Brahms. Chantelle and I played our Chopin and Tchaikovsky discs.

Each day more and more of the snow disappeared in the fields around Acton, and water filled the ditches along the road from the trailer park to school. Lynetta and Jasmine couldn't resist chasing one another through puddles, and their snowsuits always seemed to be soaked by the time we got home in the afternoon.

I was busy turning these in front of the furnace vent in the kitchen one afternoon when there was a knock on the door. Ashley and Holman raced each other to open it.

"Who is it?" Kitaleen called from the living room.

"Chantelle…" Holman shouted back.

"Hey!" I hurried to the door.

It wasn't only Chantelle. Malcolm and Amber stood behind her. I could see Malcolm had a pile of pizza boxes in his arms and Amber was holding a case of pop.

"Hey!" My voice was stuck on the word.

Kitaleen hobbled to the doorway between the living room and the kitchen.

"Bless my soul!" she said. "What a surprise. Come on in! It's Amber, isn't it, and…?"

"Supper's on us tonight," Malcolm said cheerily as he introduced himself.

Once we had the pizzas set out, I kept waiting for Mike to show up, and I think both Kitaleen and I heaved a sigh of relief when five-thirty came and passed.

"I saw your dad at Metro's when I picked up the pizza," Malcolm said to Ashley, who was pouring root beer into glasses.

When we'd eaten the pizza, Amber and Malcolm pretended to have a scrap over who was going to wash and who was going to dry the dishes. Kitaleen retreated into the living room where she had Chantelle trying on the fairy puppet gloves.

It was the happiest I'd seen Amber in a long time. As I made sandwiches for the next day's lunches, I couldn't help watching them. They were like teenagers in a Sears flyer, with skin that seemed to glow and hair that picked up overhead lights. They wore perfect clothes. Malcolm was snapping a tea towel at Amber, and she began chasing him around the table. Jasmine and Lynetta joined the chase and piled on Malcolm.

"Hey, I give," Malcolm laughed. He picked up Lynetta and tickled her until she squealed.

"Me, too," Jasmine begged, and Amber picked her up and began twirling her around until they were both dizzy and laughing nonstop.

When the two little girls were bathed and in bed, Ashley and Holman hunted up the Pictionary game Gentry had brought home for Christmas. We played that while Kitaleen sewed sequins onto the hand-puppet fairies to finish them up. The little boys were both pretty good with a pencil, even if they didn't understand the meaning of a lot of the words. Holman actually got the word fairy on one of his cards. He quickly drew a hand with little faces on the end of each finger.

Everything Amber drew had Malcolm making guesses that were sillier and sillier and left her helpless with laughter. At one point, Chantelle looked over and caught my eye. I think we stopped and had a small chat in that brief look.

"Something's happening here," the look said, "and it's going to get more and more interesting when Shon figures this out."

From my bedroom window, I watched the trio as they headed for home along the trailer park road. Malcolm punched Amber playfully on the arm and the two went dashing back and forth across the road as Chantelle soldiered on in that odd little dip-and-dive way. I crawled under the covers and tried to concentrate on a story we were supposed to read for the next day.

When I gave up and switched off the light, moonlight spilled through the window, giving everything that other-world kind of look. A world of shadow and silver. I closed my eyes and saw Malcolm's face as he played with the kids and teased Amber. When he and

Amber had raced back and forth along the road home, it was almost as if there was something connecting them, like marionette strings.

I felt an ache, the kind of ache Gentry would call growing pains.

Was there another name?

Jealousy.

Fifteen

Gentry came home the week of spring break.

"Lord," she declared, as Holman and Ashley lugged her suitcases in from the van. "I feel like the floorboards of the Silver City Saloon. Like people been dancing on me for so long I'm plum wore down. Got grooves in me!"

Gentry's room was the one Kitaleen used for sewing when she wasn't home. While Kitaleen hadn't been able to sit at the sewing machine since her accident, there were bits and pieces of projects she'd been working on all over the open sewing cabinet and the bed.

"Looks like a cyclone hit Fanny's Fabrics." Gentry cleared a spot on the bed for her suitcases. I began grabbing things and hunting for places to put them. The day she fell downstairs, Kitaleen had been sewing some soft toys to sell at a craft sale in town. A half-finished Winnie-the-Pooh and a pinned-together Paddington sat in an island of pattern pieces. A shiny black skirt with white fringe tacked to it in places was draped over the dresser.

"Guess I'm going to have to wait a while for this." Gentry picked up the skirt and held it against her. Ashley and Holman had her cases set out on the bed, and Lynetta and Jasmine had filed in behind their brothers, wide-eyed.

"Well, let's see," Gentry laughed. "Which of these cases has got presents for my nieces and nephews? Why don't you snap open that spotted cowhide one, Ashley?" She doled out bits of costume jewelry to the little girls and a pile of comic books to the boys.

"Good thing they had a flea market in that Silver City Hotel the week I was there." She winked at me. "Take this down to your mama now." Gentry gave Jasmine a doll with ringlets and an old-fashioned hoop-skirt dress. "For her collection."

"So, kiddo..." Gentry lit a cigarette when we were alone. "How's it going?"

"Okay," I mumbled. "I've been tired..."

"I'm not surprised!" She gave me a little hug. "Mike ain't so broke he couldn't've hired someone to come in and help. Makes me so mad. That man's tighter than leotards at a Weight Watchers convention." She took a long drag on her cigarette. "And your play?"

"It's coming along good. Do you think you can get

some days off during grad week? We'll be having the play and a fashion show..."

"Just let me know when it is and I'll make time." Gentry shoved a Curious George off her dresser bench and sank onto it. "How's your little friend?"

"Chantelle? Kitaleen and I are going to make her grad dress for her. I drew a design for it. We're going to use the rhinestone butterflies I gave her for her birthday, and Miss Riccio–"

"Poor little thing." Gentry found an ashtray under some loose pieces of felt on her vanity table. "I hope you guys make her the most beautiful–"

"She's not a poor little thing!" I felt the hairs on the back of my neck stand up.

Gentry took another long drag on her cigarette and kicked away a mound of cotton batting resting over the toe of her cowboy boot. She gave me one of those long Gentry looks, like she was figuring something out and wondering how it could fit into the chorus of a song.

"She can't help how she looks, and she's smart..."

"Of course," Gentry said, blowing a couple of smoke rings.

"I wish you'd quit smoking. They showed us a video at school about what can happen to you. It's pretty ugly."

Gentry gave me another long look. "Well, sweetie,

how about you clear out and let your old mother freshen up a bit? She's a trailworn old chuckwagon nag at the moment."

Gentry said she'd booked off two weeks so she could help with Kitaleen's convalescence, but by the end of the first week she decided to head back to the city. I could see being at home with Kitaleen and the kids was more than Gentry could handle.

"My cloth ain't cut in a housework pattern," she told me the evening before she left again. We were having hamburgers at Metro's. Her end-of-visit treat. "Lord, I hope we don't run into Mike. Kitaleen says he's practically living here these days. Though I can't say I blame him."

My mouth dropped open.

"Oh, you know what I mean," Gentry laughed. "Mike's no more domestic than I am. Give me three days of washing floors and wiping noses and cooking tuna casserole and I'm ready to join a bowling league myself."

"I'm glad he's not around much. But I wish you were here more."

"You're sweet." Gentry wiped a little hamburger relish off her chin. "You'd probably change your mind if I was here longer than a week. Anyway, things'll be easier next week when you go back to school. I'm hiring Mrs. Weigle to come in for a couple of hours a day to help with the housework. Remember, you used to call her Mrs. Wiggly when you were wee small and she lived in that trailer next to us?"

Gentry finished her hamburger and lit a cigarette.

I gave her a stern look and she laughed.

"Just don't tell Mike I'm paying for Mrs. Wiggly," she said. "I want him to think he's going to have to."

After the break, it seemed like all the grade nine teachers had taken a deep drink of year-end-exam-seriousness medicine. Words like review and rubric and buckle down hung in the air.

We did have our last set of options for escape. Miss Riccio was teaching a module called Enterprise and Innovation, which Malcolm, Chantelle and I all managed to get into. Miss Riccio said she'd figure out some way to make playwrighting, puppet-making, music composition and production fit into it, so the three of us could continue working on *A Midsummer Night's Dream.*

Amber, at Shon's insistence, was taking Foods from Mrs. Parkerhouse, our grade nine language arts teacher who'd got stuck teaching it.

"She generally blows up at least once a period," Amber told us. "Takes turns crying and yelling. Shon and the other guys just laugh. I'm trying to get them to be nice..." Her voice trailed away.

Later, when we were alone, Chantelle told me that Amber had tried to break up with Shon and he'd gone ballistic.

"He smashed up the Walkman she'd given him for Christmas, and a piece of the broken plastic cut his arm. Then he started to rub the blood on her. Amber was crying when she told me about it and I thought she'd never stop."

"Did he hurt her?"

"No. Just got blood all over her sweater."

I looked at Chantelle. I didn't have to ask the question.

"I think she's too scared to leave him right now. I told her she's got to."

"Not easy," I said. "Having Shon love you may be as bad as having Shon hate you."

A cold, dreary April slipped away as we began reviewing the core subjects and putting together the parts of our grad play that would make it a "spectacle of incredible magnitude" (we were learning to identify the language of advertising in language arts and borrowed what sounded good).

In early May the weather changed. A week of days as warm as midsummer turned Mavis Buttley's hallways into a sea of T-shirts and shorts. Classroom windows were pried open. Mrs. Parkerhouse took us outside to write metaphors and similes, a fiasco that ended up with her running around the ball field screaming at Shon Docker and Cameron Coaldale, who were chucking bits of fungus at everyone.

Shon Docker, Chantelle wrote in her notebook, *is as sensitive as a hunk of moldy tree fungus. Simile.*

Cameron, a moraine, a neolithic deposit, I wrote in mine. *Metaphor.*

We saw Mr. Stambaugh coming across the field toward us. Shon and Cameron and Mrs. Parkerhouse saw him at the same time we did and it was funny how all three suddenly changed into what they were supposed to be – a teacher and two students. Everyone watched to see what kind of a dressing-down Mr. Stambaugh would give the boys. But it was Chantelle and me that he came over to.

"Chantelle, I'd like to see you in my office if you don't mind coming back to the school now." Mr. Stambaugh wiped his forehead with the handkerchief from his suit pocket.

It was odd watching the two of them go back across the field to the school, Mr. Stambaugh trying to walk beside Chantelle instead of three steps in front of her. Even at a fairly slow pace, she was having trouble making it across the spring roughness of the ground. She nearly fell by the baseball backstop, and the principal swooped his long arms down to steady her.

As we straggled back into the school ourselves a few minutes later, I noticed Mr. Stambaugh's big black sedan pulling out of the school driveway. It almost looked like he was driving by himself. I could just see the very top of Chantelle's head in the passenger seat.

Malcolm grabbed me by the arm as we headed to our lockers to get our books for math class.

"Chantelle's dad died," he said.

"You're kidding."

"No. Wilburson told me." Mr. Wilburson was the Mavis Buttley custodian. He knew things before anyone else in the school.

"It's true," Kitaleen said when I got home. "I was in the clinic this morning for my leg checkup and just before I was supposed to go in, Dr. McTavish hightailed it over to the dorm like it was on fire again. It took me a minute to get over to the window, but I could see Eva running down the walk to meet him. Did you know she's a white blonde these days?"

"I'm going to phone Chantelle."

"You go ahead and call her," Kitaleen said. "Mrs. Weigle made a casserole for supper and all I have to do is pop it in the oven. So if you want to go over…"

The first three times I tried, though, the phone was busy. Then Malcolm called me.

"It was a stroke," he said. "Dad said it wasn't any surprise. Don't tell anyone, but it looked like he'd been dead for quite a few hours. Maybe since early last night. I guess Chantelle's mom – you know – doesn't sleep in the same room."

When I finally got through to the old dorm, a man's voice said, "Yeah, she's up in her room but I'll see if she wants to talk to you."

"Hiya." It was a barely audible whisper.

"Are you okay?" I asked.

"Sure." There was a pause. "I just feel odd, I guess. And the upstairs seems so quiet. I keep waiting to hear him cough or blow his nose."

"He's been sick a long time."

"I can't remember when he wasn't sick," she said. "I used to think how nice it would be to have a father like Alison McTavish's – someone who did things with his kids. I'd see Alison and her dad hand in hand in the park or rushing off to her dance lessons..."

"Yeah, I know what you mean," I sighed. "We're a couple of part-time orphans, I guess."

"Changeling children."

"Do you want me to come over?" I asked.

"Sure," Chantelle said. "If you want to get in on one hell of a party."

Sixteen

It was a party that lasted until the day of the funeral. Each time I stopped by to see Chantelle, I noticed her backyard had sprouted more and more motorcycles and pickup trucks as her brothers came home.

Chantelle hadn't seen a few of them in years. Jimmy and Aaron had moved to Vancouver Island when she was in grade three. I could see she was embarrassed by the big fuss they were making over her. Granger, who worked in a diamond mine in the Northwest Territories, hadn't been home in two years. He was the quietest of the boys, the one who seemed most aware that Chantelle was fifteen, even if she wasn't much bigger than an eight-year-old.

"Hey, sport!" Randy gave me a slap on the back. The red fuzz on his face had grown into a thick, curly beard since our birthday party. He looked as much like a Viking warrior as a biker. A Viking warrior in a leather vest and leather pants. "Y'know, 's nice of you to come over 'n' be with Chant..." Both he and

Dwayne looked like they were well along the road to total drunkenness.

"Old man had his faults." Dwayne cornered us, weaving unsteadily with a bottle of beer in one hand and a cigarette in the other. "But I seen worse. Only gave me a licken one time..."

Chantelle was tugging at my sleeve.

"Jus' one time." Dwayne stopped to belch, setting his beer down for a minute to pound his barrel chest. "An' tha's pretty good 'cause I got in enough trouble to get a licken or two a week. Randy, you remember when – "

"Don't tell me!" Chantelle gave a little squeal. "You'll be starting me down the road to crime."

Randy stopped, perplexed for a minute, and then, roaring with laughter, picked Chantelle up as if she were a toddler.

"Rando!" Chantelle screamed. "Put me down!"

"Lord's sake, put her down!" Eva Boscombe moved unsteadily across the room. "Not that I guess we need to worry 'bout the noise no more."

Chantelle gave Randy a small kick as he set her back down. It made me think of Tinker Bell taking on Captain Hook.

"We're jus' missin' Wiley," Eva Boscombe confided to me. "Jimmy's gonna check 'n' see if they'll give him, you know..."

Chantelle raised her eyebrows. "Spring him?"

"Give him...passionate leave." She shook her head to make the word sort itself out. "*Com*passionate leave. Then I'd have my whole family."

Suddenly she staggered, as one of her high-heeled pumps gave way. Both Randy and Dwayne reached out to catch her, creating a small rainstorm of beer.

"Why don't I get you your slippers, Mama?" Chantelle said.

"Oh, honeypie, that's a good idea. Before your poor old mother falls over on these. I jus' put 'em on 'cause Ed always liked to see me dressed up." She kicked off the pumps and sighed as Randy held onto her arm. "We are slaves to fashion, Travis, an' tha's the truth."

Eva had her heels on again for the funeral. It had rained the night before, and as Ed Boscombe's casket was lowered mechanically into the ground, his wife's black patent pumps sank in the soft soil. I hoped that Chantelle wasn't noticing this. She was standing next to Jimmy, who had hold of her hand.

The sight of Eva struggling to keep from tilting backwards as her stiletto heels sank was causing a horrible giggle to form somewhere inside me. I knew I had to keep it from escaping. I made myself look at other things. Polished granite headstones and wooden crosses and a couple of white marble ones with baby lambs sculpted on them. Grandma's gravestone, the color of a cloudy day. There were raised letters on it that said Alice Holman, Beloved Wife and Mother.

"I wish Mike would've got home so I could have gone." Kitaleen wanted to know all the details of the funeral service and the graveside ceremony and what the United Church ladies had served for lunch back at the church hall. "Wonder what Eva'll do now? Hardly seems worthwhile for her and Chantelle to be rattling around all by themselves in that big old dorm."

Since the news about Ed Boscombe, Kitaleen had been putting extra energy into working on Chantelle's grad dress. "Maybe it'll cheer her up when she sees how gorgeous it is."

Chantelle did seem to perk up when she tried on the dress, even if it was mostly tacking stitches that held it together. The material was a black, silk-like synthetic that seemed to shimmer with dark blue undertones. I'd consulted with Miss Riccio and come up with a design that consisted of a loose cowl and capelike overtop, and a skirt that fell to the floor in a cascade of irregular overlays.

When Chantelle put it on, the gown hid her own irregularities of design.

"Hey!" she said, looking at herself in Gentry's full-length mirror in the sewing room. "Way to go, Stitchmaster!"

"Now imagine," I said, "rhinestone butterflies settled into the folds, plus some little bead-and-sequin stars here and there. Kitaleen and I have it all worked out."

"Am I ever glad I bought you that pack of underwear when we were in grade five," Chantelle said softly, unable to take her eyes off the mirror.

During the last week of May, Shon Docker turned sixteen. He missed three days of school and then turned up finally in front of Mavis Buttley with his own car, an old Toyota that had sat in someone's front yard with a 4 SALE sign in its window over the winter. Shon had turtle-waxed its red surface to a blinding brightness.

"Kind of like giving a can of gasoline and a box of matches to a pyromaniac," Malcolm observed. We were basking in the continuing May sun on the front steps of the school.

"Terror on wheels," Chantelle agreed.

Cameron, Todd and Amber spilled out of the vehicle. As other kids clustered around Shon's showpiece, she gave us a quick flutter of her hand.

During our noon-hour practice for *Dream*, Amber showed up breathless, her face flushed, apologizing for being late.

"Hey," Malcolm said, "good timing! We're just doing the lead-in to Hermia."

I caught a note of disappointment in his voice. He'd already done the introductory song, something he'd finished this past week to set the mood for the play. Both Mrs. Dahlbeck and Miss Riccio had applauded loudly and the students there for practice had joined in.

I'd just begun the dialogue in Act One between the Duke of Athens and Hermia's father. With a puppet on each hand, I was shouting – using a deep voice for the duke and a high, whining voice for Hermia's father.

Amber slipped the Hermia puppet onto her hand. She was getting better at using her pleading voice, begging her father to refuse Demetrius and let her marry Lysander.

Malcolm was playing the two suitors, so he had to move from the keyboard and get one on each hand. Miss Riccio had suggested giving them brightly colored hats so the audience could keep track of them. Lysander's was red velvet with a ruby cut-glass brooch of Miss Riccio's. Demetrius's was green with a couple of chicken feathers we'd managed to dye green.

Chantelle was doing Helena, Hermia's rival. As a contrast to Hermia's dark hair (made from strands of unraveled wool from an old black sweater), I'd made Helena's bright yellow.

Chantelle's high, airy voice brought the first act to a close:

O teach me how you look, and with what art
You sway the motion of Demetrius' heart!

Malcolm provided a flourish of electronic music and everyone clapped again.

"It's coming together," Mrs. Dahlbeck exclaimed loudly.

As we got out the puppets for the scene with Oberon and Titania, I heard Amber whisper to Chantelle, "I wish Shon would grow up."

"What did he do?"

"Oh, you know." Amber was fitting on the multiple-fairy gloves that Kitaleen had finished. "Just always goofing..."

"Yeah?"

"Like he knew when our practice started and that's when he decides to go for a drive. I had to beg him to bring me back."

Malcolm was back on his keyboard with a song – "Over Hill, Over Dale" – to introduce Act Two. Amber wasn't in it until later so she drifted over beside Malcolm, her finger-fairies keeping time to the beat of the song.

When Chantelle and I went over to Malcolm's place after school a few days later, he kept checking out the kitchen windows as we got our nachos and cheese and soft drinks.

"She said for sure she was going to try and get here," Malcolm said.

Chantelle and I gave each other the eye.

"It's not that easy to shake Shon," Chantelle said. "And now that he's got wheels..."

"He can't imagine anyone choosing to do something other than ride around with him." I finished Chantelle's sentence. "I wish she'd just give him the old heave-ho."

Malcolm turned away from the window and looked at me as if I'd suddenly raided a secure zone in his thoughts. "Hey, want to see what I'm wearing for grad?"

In his room, he pulled a hanger from his closet. He'd taken a trip into Edmonton with his dad and mom the weekend before. A suit bag had the words Holt Renfrew on it. Even the printing looked expensive. Malcolm let the Holt Renfrew cocoon slip away, revealing a dark charcoal jacket and trousers, and a shirt that looked like it had been spun out of silver.

"Wow – a suit," Chantelle reached out and touched the soft, smooth cloth. Not many grade niners got suits for grad. Dress pants and a vest were pretty much the uniform.

"Model it for us," Chantelle said.

"A sneak preview?" Malcolm laughed. He slipped the silver shirt over his T-shirt and began to unbuckle the belt on his jeans. "Turn around, Chantelle."

"Or I could just close my eyes," she smiled.

"No, the temptation to peek would be more than your mortal soul could bear." Malcolm winked at me. There was a flash of naked legs and Calvin Kleins as he got into the new trousers. I found myself looking away, heat rising to my cheeks.

"Okay, you can look." He began strutting across his room as if he were a model on a runway. "Wait, we need music." He punched a button on his sound system and loud bass-driven music began thudding an accompaniment. Malcolm did a mock twirl and took off his jacket, trailing it behind him. Both Chantelle and I watched with a bit of horror. Neither of us were used to floor surfaces that wouldn't have left a cargo of dust.

"You'll slay them," Chantelle said. "All the girls will fall in love with you and all the boys'll be green with envy."

When I got home, I checked the box under my bed where I'd packed away my own outfit for grad. Gray pants from Zeller's, but not bad, and a cotton turtleneck Gentry had given me for my birthday. The vest I'd sewn, with some help from Kitaleen, was what made the outfit something more than a Zeller's flyer special. It was a darker gray than the trousers, heavy material that we'd lined with dark cotton. Against the dark gray I'd stitched an abstract design that covered the entire vest, giving it a texture that was a little like the markings on tropical reptiles. When I showed it to Chantelle, she called it a gila-monster vest.

I tried it all on for about the hundredth time and went into Gentry's room to see myself in the full-length mirror. Kitaleen hobbled in with a half-finished Tigger toy. She was getting ready for another craft sale.

"Well, it's still like climbing Mount Everest to get up here to the sewing room," she laughed. The cast had been gone for a couple of weeks. Mike had added another handrail to the steep stairway, so there was one on each side now.

"My, you look handsome." Kitaleen sank onto Gentry's bed. "I bet you're going to be the best-looking boy at grad."

"Actually, no," I said. "That would be Malcolm McTavish."

Seventeen

We'd waited so long for grad week that when it finally came, it was as if the days were suddenly tripping and falling into one another. Everything was moving too fast as we worked to get all the parts of the play fitted together. The fashion show run-throughs, with commentary and music, had to be scheduled so they didn't conflict with rehearsals for *A Midsummer Night's Dream*, since so many students were in both. Then there was the prep for the grad ceremony itself and the dance at the end of the week.

Mrs. Dahlbeck did what Malcolm called her fireworks special at the first dress rehearsal for *Midsummer*, screaming at the "zingers" for coming in late on cue and failing to project their voices.

"You will not be heard past the first row," she yelled. "All this work and to have it sit on the stage and go nowheres. Just because you will not open the mouths!"

The night of the play, the gym was packed. Our puppet stage looked like Vistavision stretching across the stage. Miss Riccio had sweet-talked Mr. Johnson into having a couple of his students build it as a woodworking project. I'd had to add a couple of panels to my black velvet curtain so it would cover the long opening.

As people filed in and found their seats, a spotlight played against the design of leaves and stars and the crescent moon I'd embroidered. The musicians and choir were in position at the sides of the puppet stage. Chantelle, Amber and I sat beside them. When the room darkened, we would take our places behind the puppet stage where hidden lights let us see the puppets on their hooks, all arranged and ready for our hands. We knew our lines pretty well but it was good to see scripts on a couple of clipboards, just in case.

Gentry, Kitaleen and the kids were in the second row. I tried to pretend I couldn't see Lynetta and Jasmine waving at me. Gentry blew a kiss. I made a quick flutter of fingers in their direction, hoping my face wasn't turning too red. The McTavishes were out in full force. Malcolm's parents and his cousin's parents, and even grandparents who'd made the trip from the city.

"Are your mom and dad here?" I whispered to Amber.

"Hiding in the back somewhere," Amber said. "My dad always likes to be at the back of things."

As the gym lights went down, I noticed Eva Boscombe slipping in and a student usher hunting for a seat for her.

The hush as the auditorium went dark and we pulled back the curtain gave way to a little "ooh" when the string of Christmas fairy-lights glittered across the top and base of the opening and Amber displayed her ten finger-fairies dancing and flitting here and there. Malcolm played something on his keyboard that sounded like music notes pouncing, trying to catch the fairies, and then the sound grew slower and slower and the finger-fairies appeared to fall asleep against one another. With a voice like soft velvet, Malcolm sang the lines of his opening song:

> *Welcome night*
> *and dream away the time —*
> *Herald the moon, a silver bow*
> *new-bent in heaven.*
> *Dream a tale of lovers caught,*
> *lost to reason, lost to rhyme —*
> *lost to reason, lost to rhyme.*

As the song faded, there was a wave of applause. My heart seemed stuck in my throat as I got the duke and Hermia's father onto my hands.

"My gracious duke," I whined loudly and heard a faint echo from the microphone clipped onto my collar. "My daughter will not marry with Demetrius."

The play began.

At intermission, we made our way out to the foyer where some of the grade eights who were taking the entrepreneurship course had set up a refreshment stand, selling pop and coffee and Rice Krispie squares. Kitaleen was doling out drinks and squares to the children.

"Travis!" she called to me, sputtering bits of Rice Krispie. "It's wonderful! And Chantelle...you're so, well, funny. I swear I had tears streaming down my face."

Chantelle smiled, catching onto my shirt to keep her balance in the crush of people.

"Gentry's gone outside for a smoke," Kitaleen said, "and your mom's out there, too, Chantelle."

We made our way through the crowd to the door and out onto the front steps. About a quarter of the audience was out there getting their nicotine fixes.

"Lord," Gentry laughed, giving me a hug, "I always thought Mr. Bill Shakespeare was like drinking a mug of Buckley's Mixture, but you guys have made it as sweet as...I don't know what....sweet and tasty as Kitaleen's marshmallow cherry delight. What d'you say, Eva?"

Chantelle's mom exhaled a small cloud of smoke. "Fantastic!" It seemed for a minute that she was trying to find something to add but then settled for the one word. "Fantastic, honey," she repeated and patted Chantelle on the head.

"It meant taking some days off right in the middle of the best gig we've had since Christmas," Gentry said, picking up on a conversation she must have been having with Eva Boscombe. "But I said I wasn't going to miss this even if they offered to fill my cowboy boots with pure gold..."

"See you after," I said. "We need to go back and get ready."

When we crept back behind the puppet theater, Amber and Malcolm were already there, and I had a feeling that they'd been sitting close together, moving apart as they heard us coming. We gave each other high fives all around. The gym lights went off and on a couple of times and then we were into our second half.

Malcolm had the whole audience laughing as he sang loudly, braying off-key as Bottom when he is transformed into a donkey. The puppet head was one that Miss Riccio and I had labored over so that the donkey's upper muzzle could move in a different direction from his bottom jaw. We'd given him crossed eyes and gigantic donkey ears.

As Titania, Chantelle lisped her words of love and praise into the donkey's oversized ear:

> *I pray thee, gentle mortal, sing again:*
> *My ear is much enamored of thy note.*

I heard a longing and wistfulness I hadn't noticed before. Was everyone falling in love with Malcolm?

A Midsummer Night's Dream is filled with people yelling at each other as Puck does his mischief and gets everyone to fall in love with the wrong people. I think we were all getting hoarse by the end of the last act. Even Malcolm. It was a relief to him that the choir picked up Puck's song in the finale while he was back on the keyboard:

> *If we shadows have offended*
> *Think but this, and all is mended:*
> *That you have but slumbered here,*
> *While these visions did appear.*
> *And this weak and idle theme,*
> *No more yielding than a dream —*
> *No more yielding*
> *   than a dream.*

We closed the curtains to thunderous applause. I felt tears mixing with the sweat on my face. It looked to me like Amber and Chantelle were crying, too.

Malcolm played a reprise of the opening moonlight theme as we had the puppets take their curtain calls while we stayed hidden. And then Amber, Chantelle, Malcolm and I, with puppets on our hands and others peeking out of pockets, or stuck with Velcro onto our shoulders, took a bow along with the choir and the musicians.

I remembered how the class's applause for *Peter Pan* had been the start of this. I felt a spiraling of energy in the clapping and shouts, the way I saw a bright flower opening up once in a movie where some patient photographer had taken a few frames of film every hour for a couple of days.

Miss Riccio had worked it out with Malcolm's parents to have the cast party at Malcolm's house. Pizza and pop and loud music. Miss Riccio danced right along with the rest of us. In slacks and a summer sweater and her hair tied back, she looked like a school kid herself. I had never seen Malcolm so wound up. When he danced, it seemed like he became part of the music, laughing and singing along to the lyrics.

Chantelle even got up and swayed to the music for a couple of dances when Malcolm asked her to.

"How come you never dance with me?" I asked through a mouthful of pizza when there was a break in the music.

"You never asked me," Chantelle said.

Actually it was the kind of dancing where it was hard to tell who was dancing together – everyone just moving to the music and having a good time. I noticed that both Amber and Melanie Ozipko danced as close as they could to Malcolm, though.

"Melanie might as well put her glasses back on and look for someone else," Chantelle whispered to me.

"What do you mean?"

"Amber finally did it. Dumped the Docker."

"Yikes!"

"Double yikes," Chantelle murmured.

As Chantelle and I left the McTavish house and headed to the old dorm, we noticed a red car cruising along the street, its window-glass winking as it passed under streetlights. It went to the intersection by the high school, made a U-turn and came back toward us.

We gauged how far it was to Chantelle's house and quickened our pace. Chantelle grabbed hold of my arm but even so she came close to stumbling a couple of times before we got to her gate. She did drop her tote bag once.

"You should've left the tea cozy at home," I hissed.

We'd just managed to close the gate as the car pulled up. Shon stuck his head out his open window and hollered, "Didn't you know there's a law? All freaks off the street by nine o'clock."

We turned our backs and hurried up the walk.

"Freaks!" Todd Wingate shouted.

As we got to the front door, Shon suddenly gunned the engine and took off, spewing gravel.

Eighteen

Miss Riccio tried to convince Chantelle to wear the dress Kitaleen and I had made for her in the fashion show. But Chantelle kept saying no way. I'm sure Miss Riccio figured out that she didn't want to have the world focusing on her odd, lurching walk even if she did have a gown to die for. She was just doing her teacher thing, trying to help Chantelle have more confidence in herself.

Eva Boscombe spent about an hour fussing with Chantelle's hair and helping her put on make-up. All this was happening in Eva's bedroom upstairs over our lunch break while I nibbled on a sandwich downstairs and tried to study for the math exam we'd be writing in a couple of weeks. Mavis Buttley always made sure graduation fever was over before students sat down to their finals. Math was my worst subject, and I carried the text around with me a lot, hoping something would somehow seep into me if I held the book close.

I gave up and wandered around the big living

room, stopping regularly in front of a cracked mirror that hung beside a wedding photo of Ed and Eva. The mirror was quite high, so all I could check was my rainforest reptile vest to see if it was lying the way it should against my sweater. And my hair. I could check to see if it was still gelled into place. I wouldn't apply fresh Clearasil to the zit on my chin until just before heading back.

When they finally came downstairs, Chantelle said, "I think I'm going to be sick."

"Oh, honey," Eva gushed, patting a curl of Chantelle's dark hair into place, "you look really beautiful. Doesn't she, Travis? No one's going to have a nicer dress than yours, honey."

For a couple of seconds I was speechless. Eva's cosmetic arts had given Chantelle a kind of glamorous look. She'd accented the violet of her eyes with eyeshadow and darkened her eyebrows and lashes slightly. Somehow she'd managed, with pale lipstick and lip gloss, to make Chantelle's mouth less noticeable. When she moved, the dark layers of the dress shifted and shimmered, revealing her neck, a flash of bare arm, the glittering rhinestone butterflies.

We heard the sound of motorcycles roaring into the yard, their edgy coughing and sputtering as the motors cut. Eva hurried down the hall to the back door.

"Oh, good," she called back to us. "The boys can give you guys a ride to school."

I could see that Dwayne and Randy were amazed with Chantelle's transformation. Randy was about to give me his customary slap on the back but stopped midway, checking the grease on his hands.

"Is Dad's car gassed up?" Dwayne asked. "Randy better take a shower before anyone gets too close to him."

"Yeah, you go ahead." Randy reined his hands in to his sides. "I'll get cleaned up. When is it everything gets started? Two o'clock? Should be able to get some layers of dirt off by then."

We had communication technologies first thing in the afternoon.

"I know it'll be useless to have you doing anything productive, plus only half the class is here. So, you have my permission to play computer games – Solitaire, Jigsaws – whatever your hearts desire. Work two to a station if you want." Mr. Foss picked up his coffee mug and headed out the door.

"Shon's not here," I whispered to Chantelle, who'd joined me at my computer station, still looking a bit lost and awkward in her finery. "This day's getting better and better."

At two o'clock everyone assembled in the gym. Students in the front rows, families in the back. I spotted Kitaleen and Gentry as we filed in.

Mrs. Dahlbeck's choir was on the stage, leading the program with "O Canada," and then Mr. Stambaugh began speaking into the microphone. At first we couldn't hear anything and then the sound system made a couple of high squeals while Mr. Foss hurriedly adjusted dials on the equipment at the side of the stage.

"...over a year that's been especially...er...special." Mr. Stambaugh's voice began high and then found its register. "It's been a year when Mavis Buttley has maintained its high academic standard, our hockey and ringette teams have come close to getting the county trophies, and – as you know from earlier this week – it's been a year when our drama and music have, well, dazzled everyone." There was a smattering of applause. "Now...er...we're in for a real treat..." He stammered on for a few minutes more before Miss Riccio came forward to do the commentary for the fashion show.

The senior fashion studies class had been making outfits for the summer holidays. Malcolm and Kevin Albertson got wolf whistles when they came onstage wearing brightly patterned swim shorts. Amber and Alison McTavish looked like professional models as they strutted summer dresses across the stage. Amber had been practicing walking in high heels for the past couple of weeks.

I'd checked as we came into the gym to see if Shon was with the students in his home room, but he hadn't shown up.

"Everyone's saying he's out to get Malcolm – probably Amber, too," Chantelle told me. I'd been hearing the same comments. "Dead meat, both of them," one of the grade eight boys had announced in the washroom.

Cameron Coaldale hadn't shown up either for the afternoon but I could see Todd Wingate. He made a gagging sound when Malcolm and Amber walked out together at the end of the fashion show in their grad outfits. Not that Malcolm's had been made by the fashion studies class, but Amber had made hers with quite a bit of help from Miss Riccio. Apart from Todd's feeble gagging, a little "oooh" ran through the assembly like a spring breeze. Amber's coppery hair matched the color of her dress, the fabric torn in places and then restitched with gold thread and seed pearls.

The fashion show was followed by a couple of songs from the choir. Malcolm slipped into place with the tenors and I could hear his voice over the others. It sent a tingle along the back of my neck.

This was followed by Mr. Stambaugh and Mrs. Garber, a grandmotherly woman on the school board who was a daughter of the real Mavis Buttley, handing out diplomas. The audience had been asked to hold its applause, but when Chantelle made her way across the stage like some strange, exotic little bird, there was a burst of spontaneous clapping.

There were a few hours before the dance was to begin. The conference room at the Acton Hotel had been booked after the grad committee had complained that a dance in the school gym was an insult to everyone who'd put out the bucks for shoes to go with their grad outfits. The school board's rule about gym shoes or socks only was way up there somewhere with the Ten Commandments.

Kitaleen invited Chantelle to come for supper but Eva had bought tickets for the buffet dinner the hotel was hosting before the dance.

"She looked wonderful," Gentry reported to Mike, who'd managed to make it home for Kitaleen's grad supper for me. "You'd have been proud of what Travis and Kit did to make that poor little girl look like a prom queen."

"Miracles never cease," Mike allowed through a mouthful of spaghetti. "Is that what kids are wearing for good these days?" He waved his fork in my general direction. "White shirt an' tie a thing of the past?"

"As if you wore white shirts and ties when you were his age." Kitaleen dished herself a second helping of meat balls. "You don't remember those puffy-sleeved, big-collar things that looked like wallpaper pattern?"

For once Mike grinned.

"Travis's outfit looks positively tasteful when I think of what guys used to deck themselves out in twenty years ago."

"That's why I like cowboy style," Gentry said, already into her coffee and cigarette course. "It doesn't change every time some guy in Paris or New York decides hemlines got to go up or down or people should start wearing their undies outside their regular clothes."

Gentry's show outfits were on hangers by the kitchen door, ready to be loaded into the van. She was headed back to the city once supper was over.

"It'll save me traveling the same day I'm doing a show," she'd decided. "Plus you don't want your old mother hanging around when you're out gallivantin'. Time flies by faster 'n a toad snapping up a blackfly for breakfast. Lord, it seems..."

She didn't finish the thought, and I wondered if maybe she were wishing she'd been around a bit more.

"You sit still," she said now to Kitaleen. "The ice cream cake is my treat and I'll dish it up."

"Yay! Ice cream cake!" Jasmine's eyes lit up.

"You better watch yourself, little one," Mike said,

scraping his plate, "or you'll end up as big as your mama."

"Mike, why – " Gentry sputtered.

"You're not exactly light as a feather yourself," Kitaleen said, gritting her teeth. "Gettin' a gut on you like – "

"Aah, who asked you?"

I looked at Gentry and raised my eyebrows.

"Hell's bells!" Gentry hollered a bit louder than everybody else. "Let's see if we can have our ice cream cake without a side helping of insults."

Gentry dropped me off at the hotel on her way out to the highway. She snapped open her purse and pressed a couple of twenties into my hand.

"You have a good time, sweetie," she said, reaching out to rumple my hair and then remembering it was perfectly gelled into place. She let her fingers light on my cheek. "Treat Chantelle and the others, you know, pop or whatever..."

"I will." I gave her hand a squeeze. "Safe journey." I was surprised to hear myself saying what Kitaleen always said whenever Gentry headed off. It was something grownups said to one another.

The dance had already started. A DJ with a sound system that looked like the cockpit panel of a passenger jet was chatting into the tail end of one dance piece before blasting into the next. Malcolm and Amber were dancing giddily in the middle of the floor.

I spotted Chantelle. "Want to dance?" I mouthed.

"Okay," she mouthed back.

A lot of the kids looked on condescendingly as Chantelle did some odd little jerky movements to the music. But she just smiled at me – a quick little smile that seemed to say she was going to ignore people who deserved to be ignored.

About an hour into the dance, Shon Docker showed up at the door with Cameron and Todd in tow. They were stopped by Mr. Foss, who was chaperoning the dance along with Mr. and Mrs. Stambaugh and Miss Riccio. Shon was screaming something, but whatever he was saying was lost in the loud music. A bouncer from the beer parlor showed up in a couple of minutes and the three disappeared.

"Higher than hoot owls," someone said.

"Man – totally stoned!"

Chantelle and I were watching Malcolm and Amber. It wasn't far from the Acton Hotel to their front doors, but danger doesn't need a lot of distance. And if Shon missed getting his hands on them tonight, wouldn't it simply be a matter of time until he tried again?

When the DJ took a break, I broke one of the twenties Gentry had given me and bought pops for

Amber and Malcolm and Chantelle. We toasted one another like adults at a cocktail party.

"Do you think Shon will be waiting for you?" I asked Malcolm.

"Don't forget I took karate for three years." He mimed a couple of hand chops.

"He's so stoned, I think he'd have trouble standing up much less fighting anyone," Amber said quietly, but she sounded like she didn't believe it herself.

Toward midnight the DJ announced the last dance. I thought I saw a look of relief flit across Mr. and Mrs. Stambaugh's faces, although Mr. Foss, who'd been dancing with Miss Riccio, didn't seem anxious to quit.

Mr. and Mrs. McTavish showed up just as the dance was ending.

"Thought we'd be your limousine tonight," Mr. McTavish joked. Malcolm's mom's Mrs. Brady smile was firmly in place.

"Can we give you a lift home, Travis? Chantelle?"

"Gee, thanks," I said, "but I'm staying over at Chantelle's tonight. It's just a block."

When we passed the beer parlor door on our way to the exit, someone came out and we caught a glimpse of Randy and Dwayne sitting at a table covered with foaming glasses of beer. "Hey, kiddo!" Randy yelled as the door wheezed shut again.

Chantelle and I stepped out onto the tarmac behind the hotel. It was a clear, warm night, and the sky seemed to have put on its own display of fairy lights. I thought Chantelle and I both sighed at the same moment, but maybe we were both just catching a breath after the stale inside air. In a couple of weeks we'd have the summer stretching before us and there was this problem. What to do after you've done the ultimate puppet spectacular of *A Midsummer Night's Dream*?

"You know," I said, "I'm thinking I'm ready to move on to marionettes. And maybe I'll write my own plays."

Light from the yard lamp at the back of the hotel glittered on Chantelle's rhinestone butterflies. "Just promise me..."

At that moment we both became aware of Shon Docker's car pulling up across the street from us, stopping, idling, no lights on. Then Dr. McTavish's big bronze-colored sedan rounded the corner and drove past. Shon's red car continued to purr for a couple of moments and then burst forward with lights on, engine roaring. It nearly caught up to the sedan before, like some metallic animal that suddenly abandoned its prey, it stopped suddenly. The sedan's taillights flickered and disappeared as it turned onto the next street.

Then Chantelle and I realized the red car was reversing furiously, fishtailing toward us. Before we could even think of running, it was right beside us, the doors flung open.

Shon Docker was howling with rage. "Get in, faggot. You're going for a little ride."

"No!" Chantelle's voice was a tiny, squeaky scream.

"Butt out, freak-face." Todd Wingate pushed her down. Someone was behind me and had my arms pinned. I was kicking and yelling as loud as I could as I was pulled into the back seat of Shon's car.

Cameron Coaldale breathed into my ear, "You're gonna wish you'd never been born."

Nineteen

Tires squealed, gravel flew. Shon and Todd and Cameron whooped and swore out their open windows. On the edge of town, Cameron threw a beer bottle at the Welcome to Acton sign.

"Let me out," I yelled. "I haven't done anything to you."

"Shut up," Shon snarled.

"Weren't for you, faggot, Amber'd still be goin' with Shon." Todd turned around in the passenger seat and glared blearily at me. "You and that little Ewok creep."

We drove without anyone saying anything for a few minutes. There was just the dizzying motion of the car as it moved at uneven speeds up and down hills, nipping here and there at ditches.

"Where are you taking me?" I asked Cameron. My voice came out frightened, croaking, and I could feel tears welling. God, I thought, please keep me from crying.

"Don't know," Cameron said, and then he hollered to the front seat. "Whaddya think? The pits? That's a good place for teaching faggots lessons."

Shon swung onto a side road that led to the gravel pits.

"Let me out," I begged. "I'll walk all the way home. I didn't tell Amber to break up with you."

"Yeah, and fairies don't fly with little pinkie wings!" Todd spat at me.

"Y'know…" Shon turned his head and nearly drove into the ditch, over-correcting with the wheel so we went lurching onto the entrance to a farmer's field. The car squealed and groaned as he reversed back onto the road. "Y'know, the sound of your voice makes me sick. Makes me want to puke."

"Yeah, so just shut up," Cameron muttered fuzzily. Shon suddenly jacked up the sound on the radio.

As the car slowed at the turn-off to the gravel pits, I grabbed the door handle, threw it open and tried to fling myself out. Cameron had been holding onto my vest, though, and with a power I didn't imagine he possessed, he jerked me back in. My vest was bunched up around my armpits now.

"Uh-uh, queerboy. You ain't goin' nowhere – yet."

"Cameron, please," I whispered. I could feel moisture streaming along my cheeks.

We were at the pits. The gouges in the hills were

caught in shadow, making it look like a moonscape. Shon kept the car lights on and the radio blaring but turned off the engine. Echoing the beat of the music was a pounding inside me, a frantic pounding like a wild animal inside my chest, scrambling up my throat.

"Get over there, in the lights," Shon yelled at me.

"Please," I begged. "Please don't..." Cameron pushed me into the beams. There was a hollow in the ground and I lost my balance and went down on one knee so the lights were directly in my eyes.

Shon stood between the headlights and where I crouched. He was weaving back and forth, and I realized he was finishing up a bottle the three were passing around.

When Shon lurched over and handed the bottle to Cameron, Cameron let go of me. In an instant, I rolled out of the headlights and scrambled to my feet, still blinded from the car lights. I was running as fast as I could but I couldn't see where I was going.

I felt a hand against my back, and then I was falling.

It only takes a couple of seconds to plunge from the crest of a gravel quarry to the bottom, but it seemed to me that I was flying free. A Peter Pan moment. My attackers were somewhere behind, lost in the noise of running and swearing and shifting gravel and radio rap.

Flying free.

And then my chin met with a rock at the bottom of the pit, and there was a blaze of pain along my leg. I could taste blood in my mouth, and blood from somewhere on my forehead trickled into my eyes.

As I lay there, I could hear the three getting closer, stumbling down the slope. But one of them was suddenly sick with a horrible retching sound that made my own stomach want to heave.

"Shon?" someone said fuzzily. "Y'okay?"

There was a gouge in the pit across from where I'd landed, and I could see out to the road that wound over the countryside. It seemed like some kind of gateway to freedom. I tried to move, but the pain shot through my leg again with an intensity that nearly made me faint.

This is how people die, I thought, and suddenly I was crying like a little ten-year-old on the playground. This is how people die. For me it would be face-down in a gravel pit. How long would it take them, I wondered.

With the rocks of the gravel ridge pressed into my face, I thought of Chantelle and me riding along these same bluffs with Dwayne and Randy.

I remembered Chantelle's wild little hawklike cry and the sound of the motorcycle engines, the way the sound surged and retreated.

I don't know when I realized the sound of the motorbikes was more than a flashback in my mind. Maybe it was when I used my fist to wipe the blood away from my eyes and saw lights dipping and diving over the moonscape. Even with the radio blasting, that rise and fall of sound grew louder.

Todd and Cameron must have heard it, too.

"Hey, c'mon, Shon," one of them was yelling. "Y'gotta get up."

One of them scrambled back up to the crest of the pit, and I could see him outlined against the glow of the car lights. He was screaming down, "Shon, c'mon..."

Cameron began half carrying, half dragging Shon up to where Todd was. And then there were more lights and the roar of the motorcycles was right above me. The engines cut and the bright lights of the car and the loud radio music died.

But I didn't.

I curled against the side of the hollow, the pain washing over me in waves.

A big voice was yelling, "Get over there, and don't move."

The other voice hollered out, "Travis!"

"Here!" I called, but my voice caught somewhere in my throat and rode out on a sob. "Here!"

"Trav?"

"I'm here."

Before I fainted, I was aware of the massive hulk of Randy beside me, kneeling.

"Hang in there, kid," he said. A big hand carefully brushed my hair back from the blood on my forehead.

"'kay," I whispered. Then the pain from my leg doubled back on me and it seemed like I was falling again, falling away from the pain.

When I came to I was on a gurney in the emergency room of the Acton General Hospital and Dr. McTavish was talking to me. He must have been talking to me for some time, but the first words I could understand were, "...not the greatest way to end a grad."

He had a little light and was flashing it into my eyes. I turned my head. I never wanted to have lights trained on me again.

"Hey, you're back with us." He gave my arm a squeeze. "Missed all the sewing. Six stitches in your forehead; eight along your chin." He gestured to someone just beyond the green curtain.

"Okay, Chantelle, you can talk to him but just for a couple of minutes." He busied himself getting a needle out of its plastic wrap. "I'm going to give you a shot that'll help you with the pain." He smiled wearily. His eyes and Malcolm's were the same soft green color, like the brushed cotton Kitaleen used for toy dinosaurs. "It'll make you sleep..."

Chantelle had to climb up onto a stepstool to see me. I could tell she'd been crying, rubbing her eyes so that the eye shadow and mascara had smeared. It gave her a bruised look.

"Hey!" she whispered.

"Hey," I echoed. "How'd Dwayne and Randy – ?"

"As soon as I could get up I went back in the hotel and got them."

"But how..."

"Randy said he guessed they might drive you out to the gravel pits. Oh, God, Travis... " She began sobbing.

"Hush," I said. It brought the tiniest smile. "Lucky guess." I was becoming aware of how much it hurt to talk.

"He said that's where all the hell-raisers in Acton have been going for as long as he could remember."

At some point, Chantelle must have gone home and changed. She had on a rust-colored kangaroo jacket with her tote bag slung over a shoulder.

"I see you brought..." I yawned. That hurt, too, but all of the hurt – the pain along my face, my leg – was sliding away while sleep, like some friendly fog, drifted in.

"Brought what?"

"...the tea cozy," I said. And fell asleep.

Twenty

— — — — — — — — — — — — —

Chantelle was the last thing I saw as I slipped into sleep. Malcolm was the first person I saw when I opened my eyes. Biting his lip, he gently touched the stitches on my forehead and along my chin.

"Frankenstein." My voice was hardly more than battered air.

"What?" Drawing his hand back, his fingers brushed my collarbone.

"Frankenstein."

Malcolm smiled. "You don't have any screws on the side of your head."

"Not yet."

"They're going to pay for this," Malcolm said grimly. "Dad called the RCMP after the ambulance brought you in. They picked all three of them up out at the pits. I guess Chantelle's brothers left them there to walk home. That's after they took the car keys and let the air out of Shon's tires. It's still out at the gravel pits." Malcolm pulled a box of chocolates out of a grocery bag. "These are for you, from the Dream players."

Chantelle came to visit after school. She filled me in on things I'd wondered about as I drifted in and out of sleep after Malcolm's visit at lunchtime. Randy had used his cell phone to call an ambulance. They were afraid to move me because they didn't know what injuries I might have.

"Randy and Dwayne still here?"

"No, they had to get back to work. Besides, my brothers'll do almost anything to steer clear of the Mounties." Chantelle smiled. "They high-tailed out of here as soon as they knew you were okay."

"I keep thinking...you know...what might have happened if they hadn't come..." A pain settled across my chest just thinking about it.

"Don't think about that," Chantelle said softly. She suddenly became totally interested in my cast. "I can't believe I don't have one of these on myself after Todd pushed me down. My bones must be getting stronger. The doctors always said that once I got to be a teenager..."

"Do you think Shon and Cameron and Todd will be really out to get me now?"

"I wouldn't worry." Chantelle busied herself signing my cast, bordering the letters of her name with tiny stars. "The Mounties spent all morning with the three down in Mr. Stambaugh's office. I heard that if they come anywhere near you, it's into the slammer..."

"And they haven't even had to face Gentry yet," I added.

Gentry, of course, became Tornado Gentry, whirling back to town, ready to tear into my three attackers. It was just a matter of who she could track down first. Nobody was answering the door at the Wingates' or at Benita Docker's apartment. At Cameron Coaldale's, though, she confronted Cameron's grandma, who'd been raising him since he was a baby.

"In two minutes she was howling into her hankie," Gentry fumed, fussing with things at my bedside. "Said she'd tried her best but never could do anything with that boy and, of course, it was all Shon Docker's fault. I told her things would be easier when all three of them became wards of the government with their very own accommodation — in jail cells."

Gentry pulled out her pack of cigarettes. "I suppose if I light up in here, alarms'll go off all over the place." She put the smokes back in her purse and helped herself to a chocolate from the box Malcolm had brought. "I phoned Benita Docker and told her what I thought of that creep son of hers and then she started getting mouthy with me. Had the gall to say she was going to charge Dwayne and Randy

Boscombe with assault. Can you imagine! And destruction of personal property, too."

"Shon's car?"

Gentry helped herself to another chocolate. "I guess, in addition to giving him four flat tires, Dwayne and Randy couldn't resist dropping a good-sized boulder on the hood."

Although they asked about it, the crater in the car was not the main thing the Mounties were interested in when they came to see me. Constable Calliou had a soft voice and dark understanding eyes that, in a couple of minutes, had me spilling out my whole long history with Shon and Todd and Cameron. I even found myself telling him about the shoe-polish incident, and that was something I didn't think I'd ever talk about again.

"You've been really helpful," Constable Calliou said when he was finished. "I wish you'd come to us earlier, before it went as far as it did."

"I didn't think..." I tried to find words to tell him how hard it was to figure out what to do. There had always been the feeling that telling could make things flare into something even worse.

Miss Riccio came in one day after school. She had a gift bag with pictures of Van Gogh's sunflowers on its sides.

"A get-well present." Her voice cracked as she

spoke. "I had a friend of mine do some shopping in the city."

I peeked into the bag. There were three books.

"Go ahead, look at them." One of Miss Riccio's hands lit for a minute on my own and gave it a little squeeze.

The books were all on crafting puppets and marionettes. We looked through them quickly together and then Miss Riccio settled back as much as it is possible to settle back in one of those green vinyl hospital guest chairs.

"Have you given any thought to what you'll do for high school next year?" She untangled an earring that had caught in a curl of her hair. It looked like something an Arabian princess might wear.

"You mean options?"

"I mean options other than which career and tech studies you can fit into your schedule," she said. "There's a school in the city that's a fine arts school. What if you were able to get in there?"

"You mean live in the city?"

Were there really options, I wondered as she left. Would Gentry even consider the idea? How would Kitaleen get along without me? What kind of life would it be for her with just the kids and Miserable Mike?

And Chantelle? How could I go on without Chantelle?

The same day Miss Riccio visited with her books and ideas, Gentry and Kitaleen came after supper. Kitaleen leaned over and gave me a big kiss, her hair falling soft and gold all over my face. It looked like she'd just washed and curled it.

"I've been wanting so bad to get in here to see you," she whispered. "But you know Mike. Seems like he disappears just when you need him the most." She was crying, and I could feel the struggle in myself to keep the tears back. "How could they do this?" Her hands fluttered over the ridges of stitches on my face and traced the surface of the cast along my leg.

"Honey," Gentry said, "you and Kitaleen have a bit of a visit. I'm just going across the street to get some cigarettes. Get anything for you? Some chips?"

When she left, I mentioned what Miss Riccio had told me. That made Kitaleen cry even harder.

"I won't even ask Gentry, if you – "

"Oh, heavens!" Kitaleen searched her coat for a Kleenex and then spied the box on the bureau. I noticed she was still favoring her leg as she took the few steps to reach it. "Don't mind me. Of course I'd miss you terribly, and the kids will, too, but you're going to be leaving sooner or later, and maybe… when there's people around here who can do this…"

I waited until Gentry and I were alone later in the week. For once she didn't have anything to say, at least for a few minutes. The afternoon sun splashed over the window ledge filled with cards and a couple of bouquets of flowers. In the one from Chantelle, the face of the puppet Titania peered out from a bunch of tiny gold chrysanthemums.

"Why not?" Gentry murmured. "I'm not gonna be easy about leaving you here anyway."

Twenty-One

Gentry found an inexpensive apartment a couple of blocks from the fine arts school. After the made-over kitchen that had been my bedroom in the trailer, my room in the walk-up on 106th Street seemed like the inside of a very large cardboard box. It did have a small closet, and I immediately covered the entire rear wall with hooks for my puppet family.

When I pushed back the plastic accordion door, there they were. Spikehead, Medeena and Nosewart. Peter Pan and Puck. Titania glittered in the middle, Oberon at her side.

As a going-away gift, Chantelle had given me the Walt Disney *Peter Pan* prints from Wiley's bedroom. She'd also given me a three-pack of boys' briefs, with a note that read, *Just in case...* I hung the prints on the wall above the bookshelf Gentry and I had found at a second-hand store for $7.50. The briefs went into the cartons of clothes I placed under my bed.

I made a night table out of a couple of boxes I scrounged from a convenience store and covered it with some glittery cloth left over from one of Gentry's outfits. The photo album Amber gave me fit nicely on top.

"God, I'm sorry," she said when she handed me the gift. "I feel like all this happened because of me."

Going into a flurry of picture-taking seemed to make her feel better. There's a photo of Malcolm signing my cast in the hospital. Me on my crutches in front of the trailer. Gentry posing with me by the van the day we left. These are on the last page of the album.

It begins with a picture of Chantelle and me lying on Gentry's old beach blanket — the one with the three beach boys. Then there are photos from the birthday party. I look at these often. Jasmine licking icing off a giant piece of birthday cake, bits of colored frosting in her dark hair. Lynetta trying on Randy's motorcycle helmet, only her little mouth and chin showing. Holman and Ashley posing proudly by the fall bouquet they gave Chantelle. Kitaleen holding up a fistful of Monopoly money.

I don't think I realized how much I would miss them.

And then, of course, there are all the pictures

Amber took on graduation day. There's a photo someone took of her and Malcolm just as they're ready to
go down the ramp at the fashion show. It makes me
ache, somehow, to look at it. Another shows Chantelle
with her rhinestone butterflies, her violet eyeshadow,
her dark, cloudy dress. A little half-smile. I took this
one snapshot out of the album and put it in the frame
that once held the photo of me, Val and Gentry.

The small ghetto-blaster that Malcolm gave me sits
on top of my bookshelf. He made a CD of some of his
songs, including all the ones from *Dream*, and the first
few days we were in the apartment, I played it nonstop.

Gentry has her own sound system in the living
room, blaring country and western hits whenever she's
home, which isn't a whole lot of the time. Before she
went back on tour, she made sure I'd been accepted at
the arts high school. Miss Riccio had helped me put
together a portfolio that made me sound like I was the
next wonder of the theater world. Gentry went with
me when I applied and, of course, managed to cut
through all the red tape.

The area where we live can be a bit scary sometimes. Some people call it the gang center of the city,
but the most I've had to do is dodge people working
the street and try not to trip over Safeway carts being
trundled along by bottle-collectors. It was easier once
I got my cast off and quit using crutches.

Two days after we moved, we were in court for the hearing. Shon and Todd and Cameron, at the advice of their lawyers, pleaded guilty to wrongful confinement and uttering threats – a bit of a trade-off for having the aggravated assault charge dropped. Todd and Cameron didn't end up having to go into detention, but the judge put them on probation for a year and sentenced them to about a zillion hours of community service. Shon was sentenced to six months in a youth detention center to be followed by two years' probation. All three had to write me a two-page letter of apology to be looked at in advance by the judge.

"You came a hair's breadth away from committing a brutal and senseless act of violence that could have ended in more tragedy than it did," the judge scowled at them. "And it could have earned you a life spent behind bars."

"I still think life behind bars was a thought the judge should have hung onto," Gentry muttered as we left the courthouse.

"Writing a two-page letter might be almost as hard for those three," I reminded her.

When the cast came off my leg, Gentry gave me the best gift – a laptop along with a hookup to the Internet. Right away I sent my e-mail address to Malcolm and Amber and Chantelle: peterpan@planet.eon.net.

The day before school began, Chantelle sent me a note: *I'm at Amber's. I get to use her Powerbook while she's trying to decide what to wear tomorrow. That could take a few hours. I think I'm going to wear a protective coating. Wish you were going with me. I so wish it! Be brave, Stitchmaster. Be wary. Listen for the clock ticking in the crocodile.*

I e-mailed her back right away. *Salutations, quaint spirit,* I wrote in my Shakespeare voice. *Choose a protective coating that dazzles! I will be wary. I will be brave. And I will imagine you are beside me.*

It helps to imagine that Chantelle is close by. Sometimes I think I can almost feel a little tug on my sleeve, as if she is clutching my arm to steady herself. I think she'd like Arden, a boy in my creative writing class who wears paper clips in his pierced ears. He tells me about the film script he's working on and I tell him about the puppet play I've begun to write. We have lunch together sometimes, down the street at a noodle house.

At the school no one seems to mind how different you are. One of my classmates is trying to cover his body with piercings and tattoos. Another arrives at school each day with her hair in a row of colored spikes. They are mood colors, she says. "Watch out for me on purple days."

In addition to Arden, I have made friends – two in particular. Gerard has decided he is going to be the next Versace and Manuela is taking voice and dance. She can't decide whether to be a classical singer or an actress in musicals. The three of us hang out, pooling money for pizzas and videos.

Gentry is often away on road trips and flogging a CD she finally managed to get together. One of the songs on it is about a kid who is beaten by bullies. She's called it "Stitches."

It begins:

I've threaded the needle,
Stitched his baby clothes...

When she was working on those lines, I raised my eyebrows.

"Poetic license," Gentry muttered.

Then she played through the rest of the chorus to the last lines:

But I don't have a needle
Or the thread to mend
The broken, beaten teenage boy –
The boy without a friend.
The boy without a friend.

"I have a friend," I said.

"I know." She scowled and worked through an alternate set of chords for the ending. "It's a song, not a documentary."

Although Chantelle and I e-mail each other almost every day, I miss her beyond words. I miss seeing her bobbing up and down on the other side of a clothes rack at the Goodwill store. I miss trying to match my walk to the odd rhythm of her steps. I miss her crouching next to me in the tight airless space of a puppet theater, her voice high and breathy and close.

Miss Riccio is right, I remind her in one of my e-mails. *You have options. Well, maybe getting a motorcycle isn't one of them, but leaving Acton is.*

My tote bag is coming apart, she writes. *Moving to the city to be close to a very good Stitchmaster is making more and more sense.*

I don't have to write and tell her the Stitchmaster is waiting.

ACKNOWLEDGMENTS

Many thanks to friends and family who read and responded to drafts of *Stitches*. I hope you have some idea of how helpful your comments and words of encouragement have been. A special thank-you to Dianne Madill for reviewing secondary school career and technology studies with me, and to Dr. David Candler for background on Chantelle's condition.

To my editor, Shelley Tanaka, I can only say again how lucky I feel to have you working with me. Thanks so much for your close reading and thoughtful suggestions.

I would also like to thank both the Alberta Foundation for the Arts and the Canada Council for their generous support of this writing project.